Murder at Broadstowe Manor

Jason Vail

MURDER AT BROADSTOWE MANOR

Copyright 2019, by Jason Vail

A Hawk Publishing book.

Cover design by Ashley Barber; cover photo by Jason Vail

Maps by Ashley Barber

ISBN: 9781793167378

Hawk Publishing
Tallahassee, FL 32312

Murder at Broadstowe Manor

Murder at Broadstowe Manor

Murder at Broadstowe Manor

August 1263
to
September 1263

Murder at Broadstowe Manor

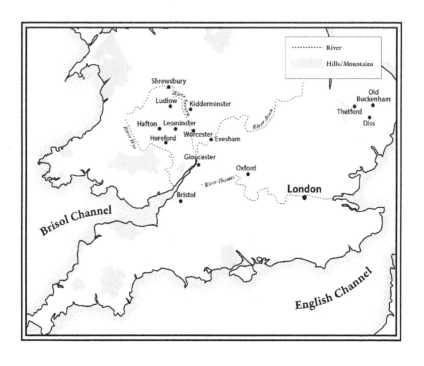

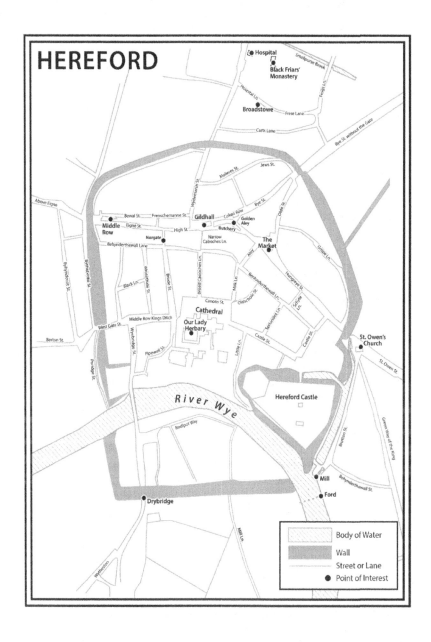

HEREFORD

Hospital
Black Friars' Monastery
Broadstowe
Smallpurse Brook
Fregis Ln.
Hospital Ln.
Frere Lane
Carts Lane
Rye St. without the Gate

Above Eigne
Jews St.
Malheres St.
Wydemarsh St.
Bewal St. — Frenschemanne St.
Gildhall
Colsan Row
Rye St.
Olde St.
Golden Aley
Middle Row — Eigne St.
Butchery
High St.
Narrow Caboches Ln.
The Market
Gosse Ln.
Behynderthewall Lane
Norgate
Alley
Behynderthewall St.
Behynderthewall Ln.
Hungrave St.
Black Ln.
Wyddefalle St.
Bride St.
Broad Caboches Ln.
Mille Ln.
Olde Schole St.
Castle St.
Sannodas Ln.
Canons St.
Cathedral
Our Lady Herbary
Middle Row Kings Ditch
West Gate St.
Wybridge St.
Pipewell St.
Little St.
Castle St.
Castle St.
St. Owen's Church
St. Owen St.
Berton St.
Pordge St.

River Wye

Hereford Castle
Rodpot Way
Berton St.
Green Way of the King
Behynderthewall St.
Mill
Ford
Drybridge
Mill Ln.
Wytherston

	Body of Water
	Wall
	Street or Lane
●	Point of Interest

9

Chapter 1

Death was not far from Stephen Attebrook's mind as he and Gilbert Wistwode entered the great hall at Hereford Castle.

Much had changed in England during the last few months, and not for the better. War was coming, many said. In fact, it seemed to have already begun. Stephen had been so preoccupied with his own business that all the political upheaval transpiring during the summer had barely registered in his mind. He had been vaguely aware that King Henry's French brother-in-law, Simon de Montfort, had summoned an army that in June marched on the Cinque Ports to prevent the further importation of foreign mercenaries by the King which were the base of his military power. Then Prince Edward had made off with most of the tax revenues of the City of London later that month and locked himself up in Windsor Castle, refusing to give back the loot since it was needed to pay his troops, while his father, King Henry, had fled to the Tower, where he thought himself safe from the rebels.

When Montfort marched toward London in July, while Stephen and Gilbert had been on the Thames chasing a Portuguese slaving ship, the City went over to him, convincing the King to make peace. So, in due course it was announced throughout the country that the King had acceded to the Provisions of Oxford and the limitations they had placed on his power. No one imagined that he was happy about it, but he did not have the support to resist Montfort, who was now the virtual ruler of the kingdom, the King a figurehead. But no peace had been made with the Prince, and it was unlikely he intended to surrender.

It was a time for choosing sides. Stephen's old enemy, Percival FitzAllan, earl of Arundel and sheriff of the county, along with many others in the Welsh March, had recently gone over to Montfort. The reason many gave was Prince Edward's seizure of the London treasury. Yet Stephen, although he owed his position as a royal coroner in Herefordshire to Prince Edward, was uncertain where his loyalties actually lay, and he wondered what he would do when the war broke out in earnest.

However, because of his appointment, most people saw him as a King's man, and it was this perceived attachment that caused him to tread with trepidation as he entered the hall.

For it was filled with adherents to Montfort's party — burghers, gentry and nobility summoned to approve the selection of delegates to a parliament Montfort had called for in October.

Stephen had no business being here, as far as he could see. But here he was.

The hall was overcrowded and noisy, since the business of the day had not yet begun, and people took the opportunity to socialize.

When people noticed Stephen, their conversation halted as they were surprised to see him here, resuming when he passed, so that it seemed a bubble of near quiet followed him until he came upon someone he knew: a neighbor of the Hafton Manor where he had grown up.

For a moment the bubble of surprise and silence held, then the neighbor, Thomas Mortimer, one of the lesser of the family of which there were dozens, said, "Well, Attebrook, come for the festivities, have you?"

"Just keeping an eye on the pulse of the county," Stephen said.

Mortimer chuckled. "It's a good idea to know which way the wind is blowing." He turned to a servant. "Fetch Sir Stephen a cup of wine, my good fellow." He went on to Stephen, "We've had an outbreak of breathing disease. How is your stock doing?"

Stephen was grateful that the talk had veered to household and manor problems, here to talk of the health of cattle — and as the lord of Hafton Manor now technically he owned quite a few — as they always did when people got together. It avoided the nettlesome subject of politics.

Gilbert, who had no interest in such matters, slipped away to fetch a cup of wine for himself, since no one was likely to do it for him.

When Gilbert returned, he stood by Stephen pretending to listen, since, as a lowly clerk and innkeeper, the highborn here were unlikely to welcome his conversation.

Stephen began to feel comfortable, and did not sense there might be anything amiss until Gilbert's eyes widened in alarm and he ducked behind Mortimer and a minor lord from near Ledbury who had overheard the conversation about the cattle problems and joined to share his own, and slipped away into the crowd.

Stephen swung around to see what had frightened Gilbert. Percival FitzAllan stood before him. The sight triggered unpleasant memories: mainly of FitzAllan having him flung into a pig sty serving as a gaol at Clun Castle, only to have it set fire by invading Welsh with him and Gilbert in it.

"So, Attebrook," FitzAllan said with exaggerated heartiness. "I am surprised to find you here!" FitzAllan was a commanding presence: as tall as Stephen but broader with massive shoulders and chest; clad in a sumptuous tunic of blue and red stitched with golden thread; knee-high leather boots of orange with silver buckles; and golden bracelets on wrists that seemed too thin to belong to those hulking shoulders; bejeweled gold rings on each thumb and little finger. His face, now sporting a short beard that ran from the bottom of his ears along the jaw to his chin, was creased with a smile.

"Why would that be, my lord?" Stephen asked. "I came at your invitation. And I have to say, I was surprised to get it."

"Did I?" FitzAllan said. "I don't recall. Must have been one of my clerks. Got his list mixed up. Happens all the time. Dunderheads, all of them. Can't trust them a bit. Well, you're here. Enjoying yourself?"

"I am, I suppose," Stephen said. But his words seemed faint to his own ears, for a woman came around FitzAllan's side whom Stephen had never expected to find here.

Margaret de Thottenham's eyes wandered across Stephen's person as if he wasn't there. She was a woman so beautiful that she could have stepped out of a painting; barely five feet tall, slender and delicate with a face that could melt any man's heart if she smiled upon him.

She took FitzAllan's arm. Stephen's heart lurched at the gesture, even though he had no right to feel jealousy. She was her own woman and did what she pleased, to the extent that did not conflict with the needs of her master, the sinister master spy Nigel FitzSimmons.

"Ah, my dear," FitzAllan said, "have you met Sir Stephen?"

"I don't believe I have," Margaret said, a lie as pure and black as the inside of a troll's cave, yet delivered in a musical voice that did not admit to doubt.

"Well, then," FitzAllan said, "Lady Margaret, Sir Stephen."

FitzAllan looked over his shoulder at someone behind him. He beckoned to that person. "While you're here, Attebrook, you may as well get the news from me."

"What news, my lord?" Stephen asked.

"We are making some changes in the county. Reorganizing things, streamlining, reducing expenses."

"I see." Stephen experienced a sense of foreboding.

"Yes, we will be eliminating the regional coroners in the county. Henceforth there will only be one." FitzAllan turned to the man who had come to his side. "Let me introduce our new county coroner, Sir Thomas de Mapuleye."

Mapuleye extended a hand. He was a small man, his head no higher than Stephen's chin, and slightly built, with brown hair flecked with gray. A receding chin and a tendency to blink gave him a clerkish air. His grasp was soft and he winced when Stephen gripped the proffered hand.

"Pleased to meet you, Attebrook," Mapuleye said, recovering his wounded hand which he massaged with the other one.

"And I you," Stephen said. "I suppose this means that I'm out."

"It certainly does," FitzAllan said. "You can go back to that little farm of yours, as long as you can keep it."

Chapter 2

"It means nothing to you, because you never liked the position, but I'm out of a job too," Gilbert said glumly. "What will I do now?"

"Chores for Edith?" Stephen asked, referring to Gilbert's wife, who was the chief operator of the Broken Shield Inn in Ludlow.

"We need the stipend. It's been a bad year, with the Welsh marauding about and all the troubles this spring and summer. Fewer people dare to take to the roads and our custom has fallen. We've had to borrow money to pay our expenses and the rent. The stipend has been the only thing keeping our heads above water, and barely doing that."

"I had no idea."

"Well, it is not seemly to talk about one's money troubles, after all." Gilbert sighed. "I wish there would be peace, but I can only see more war in our future. We'll be ruined, everything we've worked so hard for, lost."

"What happened to your share of the . . . er . . . ahem . . . you know," Stephen said, not wishing to name the subject out loud. But Gilbert would know. Earlier in the summer they had taken a chest filled with money from a Portuguese ship as it tried to flee England with his niece Ida Attebrook and a number of other kidnapped girls for the slave markets in Lisbon. Stephen's brother William had died during the attack, in which Gilbert had done his part to take it, so earning a share of the reward. "Don't tell me that's all spent."

Gilbert's glum expression became more so. "Yes."

"Not on drink and women, surely."

"I am not that sort of man!" Gilbert protested. "Bills! We have bills! Mountains of debt!"

"You bought another book," Stephen said with a flash of insight.

Gilbert's eyes got shifty.

"Admit it," Stephen said.

"All right," Gilbert said at last. "I did. Don't tell Edith."

"She doesn't know?" Stephen was shocked.

"No."

"God's blood, Gilbert, what were you thinking?"

"It is a beautiful thing! A work of art! It was going to be sold to that Philistine Sturmid de Cottenham. He'd just put it in a trunk."

"What are you going to do with it but put it in a trunk?"

"At least it shall be admired. Cottenham doesn't care a whit for beauty. He only buys such things to make himself look important."

"So you'll admire it by candlelight in the stable, I imagine."

"Well, I was going to tell Edith. I didn't think she'd mind. Then we had this financial trouble. One of our lenders called in his note, which of course we had to pay. That took the last of my share and more besides."

"And if you say anything now, she'll have your head."

"Yes. I am afraid so, as well as other parts."

There was no more that could prudently be said about this subject, so they stood in the hall surrounded by chattering people, too consumed by shock at the sudden turn of events to feel sociable.

Fortunately, FitzAllan relieved them of that burden. He mounted the dais and called for silence. "It is time for you to consider and approve the candidates whose names have been put forth to represent the county at the parliament, the good knights Sir Robert le Keu and Sir Rogier FitzHerbert! Sir Robert! Sir Rogier! Come forward!"

The crowd stirred as le Keu pushed forward and stepped up beside FitzAllan.

FitzAllan looked around for FitzHerbert but did not see him. "Sir Rogier! Where are you? Come forward!"

A murmur arose and a voice called above it, "He's not here!"

"What do you mean, he's not here?" FitzAllan asked. "How could he not be here?"

"I went by his house this morning," the voice called. "We planned to walk together to the castle. But his man said he was still in bed and not to be disturbed."

"Dammit," FitzAllan muttered. He turned to a castle steward. "Have someone fetch him!"

The ceremony of approving the representatives was put off until FitzHerbert arrived, and the chattering of gossip and socializing recommenced, subdued at first due to the embarrassment, but gradually growing in volume as people forgot about it.

Stephen and Gilbert found cups of ale and settled on a vacant bench along the wall opposite the doors. Stephen's bad foot, the one that had been partly cut off almost two years before, had begun to ache from the standing. That was his excuse, anyway, for seeking refuge against the wall. The truth was, the news he had been removed as coroner left him oddly despondent — almost as much as the fact that Margaret had taken up with FitzAllan. He had hated the job. Why should he be depressed to have lost it? Gilbert, meanwhile, had begun to look forward to dinner as a buffer to his despondency, although that was still some hours off.

"This book of yours," Stephen asked, "it's not another Gospel is it?"

Gilbert brightened at the question. "No, it's a new thing altogether from France. It's called a book of hours, *livre de la heures*, although the text is Latin. It is devotional, of course, but has masterful paintings throughout depicting events of the seasons and of scenes from the Gospels and the Psalms. It's a guide for living a devotional life." He sighed. "It's so beautiful. I have never seen anything like it."

Gilbert continued to wax enthusiastic about this book without any prompting from Stephen, who in truth was paying attention with only one ear as his eyes followed Lady Margaret as she moved about the hall. A disturbance at the doors to the hall interrupted Gilbert's soliloquy when the servant sent to collect Sir Rogier FitzHerbert rushed in shouting, "He's dead!"

The servant then hurried across the hall to FitzAllan at the dais. He rested his hands on his knees as he panted to recover his breath, as if he had run all the way across town from FitzHerbert's townhouse.

"What do you mean, he's dead?" FitzAllan demanded.

"He's hanged himself!" the servant panted.

"Hanged himself!" FitzAllan cried in return. "Nonsense!"

"It's true, lord! I saw his body myself!"

FitzAllan scowled. His fingers drummed the arm of his chair. He waved to Mapuleye who was on the floor regaling a group with some story. "Mapuleye! You're the coroner now. Go find out what's the matter."

"Hanged himself," Gilbert mused from his viewpoint on the bench. "A great lord like that! It's so unusual. I don't think I've ever heard of that happening before."

Remembering a young woman who had hanged herself from a tree last year, Stephen said, "Perhaps not that unusual. I wonder what drove him to it."

"Well, it's not our business now," Gilbert sighed.

"No, it isn't," Stephen said as he rose to his feet and strode toward the door.

"Where are you going?" Gilbert asked, hastening to catch up.

"I don't know, but I'm curious."

FitzHerbert's house was at a small manor outside the city called Broadstowe. Stephen had only a vague idea where it lay so he kept Mapuleye in sight. Mapuleye had a retinue about him, a dozen men, some of whom were burly with the look of soldiers and one with the tonsured head and black robes of a monk who clasped a writing box under an arm. These rough men were led by a red-haired man with a receding hairline and a hook nose. A large crowd of others who were curious about this unusual death often obscured Stephen's view of Mapuleye, but all he had to do was follow that crowd.

Hereford, which sat on a bend in the River Wye, was reckoned a great city, as those things were counted in England. When he was a boy, Stephen remembered hearing a burgess boasting to his father that when finished the walls would extend two-thousand-three-hundred yards. They had been completed for some years now and their U-shape, with the open end at the river, embraced a congestion of buildings that rivaled that of London, of which the burgesses were very proud.

The crowd flowed down Castle Street to Hungreye Street and through the marketplace at Saint Paul's, then down to Wydemarsh Street and through the gate into the countryside.

About two-hundred yards from Wydemarsh Gate, Mapuleye turned right down a lane running between two fields, part of them planted in barley or rye which had been reaped recently, and the other in grass, where sheep and ravens grazed.

Some distance along the lane, an imposing stone house came into view with a timber upper story at the east end.

The crowd collected about the double doors of the main entrance while Mapuleye went inside with his retinue. Servants could be seen at the windows, watching the crowd. People in the crowd shouted questions at the servants, but a senior staffer hurried the servants away and other servants pulled the shutters closed to discourage further inquiry.

The front doors opened and an imposing, square-headed man with gray hair came out onto the porch. He wore an expensive blue button-up tunic, checkered stockings, and low pointed boots that were the emerging fashion; obviously a well-to-do fellow. His expression was dignified with a hint of anxiousness. His green eyes fastened on Stephen's and he motioned Stephen to approach.

"Sir Stephen," the fellow said, "I thought I recognized you. My name is Geoffrey Curthose. I am Sir Rogier's steward. Do come in."

"I don't believe we've met," Stephen said, shaking Curthose's extended hand.

"We haven't but you've been pointed out to me and I know your reputation."

Stephen followed Curthose into the great hall. Mapuleye stood near the hearth in the center of the floor surrounded by a gaggle of men who had the look of jurors. One of them was showing Mapuleye a purple cord laced with silver thread, a noose fashioned at one end. Mapuleye stopped the explanation of what it was at the sight of Stephen.

"What are you doing here?" Mapuleye demanded. "You are relieved. You have no business here."

"Sir Stephen is here at my request," Curthose said.

"Your request. Why?"

"That is none of your affair."

"This is my affair now."

Curthose shrugged. "Perhaps the deaths are. But who enters this house is my business. Do you care to dispute me? Shall I summon her ladyship?"

Mapuleye gritted his teeth. "Just stay out of the way, Attebrook." He turned his attention to the juror holding the cord, who resumed what he had been saying.

"I suppose I must have a look," Mapuleye said to the jurymen. "You wait here."

Mapuleye ascended the stairs to the top and disappeared. He was gone a long time. When he returned he wore a troubled and thoughtful expression. His eyes swept over Stephen and Curthose, who had retreated to the raised stone dais at the west end of the hall so as not to antagonize Mapuleye any further. He seemed about to speak but thought better of it for some reason. He came down the stairs and resumed questioning the jurymen.

While Curthose and Stephen lingered on the dais, Stephen watched Mapuleye with a professional interest. The way things worked is that the jurors usually conducted the investigation, questioning witnesses, examining the body to take measurements of the wound and assess it, and the like. The jurors, who were local people, knew those involved, and the coroner often did not arrive for a day or more. As dead bodies could putrefy rapidly, especially in the warm days of summer, they were buried quickly.

"You are resolved as to the manner of the deaths?" Mapuleye asked the jurors.

"We are, I think," the noose holder said. He glanced at the others and they nodded. "Death by hanging for Sir Rogier, and murder for the boy."

"And it is your verdict that Sir Rogier killed the boy?" Mapuleye asked.

There were expressions of agreement from the jurors.

"All right, then," Mapuleye said. "Let it be so written. We will assess the rope and, I think, the bed as well. Two pounds should do it. Or do I hear a dissent?"

Again there were noises of assent rather eagerly given perhaps because FitzHerbert's estate would have to pay the fine and not their neighbors in the hundred, as was the usual case.

"Good," Mapuleye said. He headed toward the doors followed by his retinue.

"I'll take that, Ben," Curthose said to the noose holder.

Ben handed the noose over without looking Curthose in the eye.

Then he and the other jurors filed out, leaving Stephen and Curthose alone in the hall.

"Deaths, the fellow said," Stephen said. "There was more than one?"

"Yes, a servant also has died." Curthose did not provide any further explanation and Stephen did not ask for one.

"It does not seem that your lord was popular," Stephen said.

"There were rumors about him, things the neighbors did not approve of." Curthose sighed. "I'm afraid now they will know that the rumors were true."

"You did not invite me in just to hear all this."

"No. We need your help."

"For what?" Stephen asked, although he knew the answer.

"I do not believe that Sir Rogier killed the boy, or himself. He loved that boy. He couldn't have killed him. Nor do I believe he took his own life. He was a contented man with important business to conduct and such men do not turn to suicide."

"You want to save his reputation?"

"His lordship deserves to be buried in sacred ground. That cannot happen if his death is judged a suicide. As for the other?" Curthose shrugged. "The facts are the facts, and we will have to live with them."

"Why appeal to me?"

"I know your reputation for ferreting out the truth. It is said that you will not stop until it has been teased out, no matter the danger and difficulty."

Stephen, who just that morning had thought he was done with the business of death, gazed sightlessly across the hall to the tapestries on the far wall. He should just say no, but instead he said, "There will be expenses."

"I understand," Curthose said. "Whatever it costs. I will pay them even if her ladyship will not."

Chapter 3

"Ah … ahem," Gilbert ventured after Stephen had fetched him and explained what they had been asked to do, "may I ask if the bodies have been moved?"

"Who is this?" Curthose asked.

"My assistant," Stephen said.

"Hmm, well, no. I have left them in place," Curthose said.

"We should see them, and the place where they died," Stephen said.

"Very well," Curthose replied.

He led them up the stairs behind the dais table to the lord's living quarters that occupied the second story above the west end of the great hall.

There were two chambers off a brief hallway. Stephen heard voices in the one to the right: a woman's, which stopped speaking at the sound of their footsteps. Then a baby cried, and the woman spoke again soothing the child.

Curthose went to the other door, which had been battered open with an axe.

"What happened here?" Stephen asked.

"We had to break in," Curthose said. "His lordship had bolted the door."

"Did he often do that?" Stephen asked.

Curthose sighed. "Yes, I am afraid he did."

"Most unusual," Gilbert murmured, for it was out of the ordinary. Bolts on doors usually were there in case of attack to provide a last line of defense. Lords did not make a habit of bolting their doors because servants needed to gain access all the time.

"Yes," Curthose said dryly.

He pushed the door open for them and they all entered the chamber. Stephen's first impression was how magnificent it was — dark burnished wood panels carved at the tops and bottoms covered the walls. A stone fireplace occupied the far wall, no doubt the chimney shared by the other chamber. Fireplaces were rare but becoming more commonplace in the houses of the rich for the comfort they afforded within a chamber; otherwise, one shivered during the winter in unheated rooms, a reason why the servants slept around the hearth fire in the hall. There was a long table, chairs with cushions, and a carved wardrobe. Two tattered and well-worn cloaks with muddy hems hung from pegs off the wardrobe, common and out of place in such an elegant room. A large bedstead stood beside a window that admitted the sunlight through the open shutters and rendered the chamber comfortable and inviting. However, the dead — one upon the bed and the other slumped over at the foot — made the chamber less so.

The body at the foot of the bed was that of a large man lying on its side and covered with a woolen blanket. A hand with a ruby ring on the thumb and another with a yellow stone on the little finger and the feet, the legs yellowed in death with the underside a purplish color, protruded from beneath the blanket. Above the body a section of that purple and silver rope dangled from a crossbeam of the bedposts. There was a knot near where the cord had been cut, as if two segments of rope had been lashed together. It appeared to be the cord that had bound the bed curtains, for they were hanging loose and no other binding was in sight. The bed itself was a marvel of workmanship that Stephen's friend, Harry the former beggar and now a woodcarver, would have killed to get a look at: the posts were a series of animals — elephants, lions, dragons, rabbits, wolves and such in profusion — from top to bottom, with an eagle spreading its wings perched at the top of each post.

The other body, that of a young man about seventeen or eighteen, lay naked across the bed, visible only because some of the bed curtains had been tied back with plain rawhide rope.

Out of the corner of his eye, Stephen noticed a pile of clothing lying against a wall as if it had been tossed there, the large man's garments mingled with those of the boy.

Gilbert removed the blanket from FitzHerbert's body and laid it across a chair. He and Stephen knelt down beside the body, which was naked as well and lying upon the right side. There was a wet spot beside the body.

"Have you disturbed anything?" Stephen asked. "Other than cutting him down and removing the noose?"

"No," Curthose said. "I thought that prudent."

"Good thinking," Stephen said.

"Except for ..." Curthose hesitated.

"Except for what?"

"There was a mess beneath his lordship. His bowels had moved."

"I see," Stephen said. "That's all?"

Curthose nodded.

FitzHerbert must have been a handsome man in life, the face narrow, the chin strong and jutting, the nose large and narrow but not out of proportion on that large head, the brows prominent, the forehead wide; the face of a man used to getting his way, but slack now in death, the mouth open, the lips pursed and reddish from what looked like wine, the tip of the tongue protruding. The eyes were closed as if in sleep. Stephen guessed he was in his late thirties. He brushed the dark brown hair away from cheeks that could have used a shave. There was a purple abrasion upon the throat that ran around the side of the neck and climbed to the base of the skull.

"No doubt he was hanged," Gilbert said.

"How can you tell?" Curthose asked sharply as if he expected another opinion. "I am certain he was strangled. I cannot believe he killed himself."

Stephen traced the line of the abrasion with a finger. "We've seen this like before. It is characteristic of a hanging."

"The mark of a strangulation is different," Gilbert said, rising and bending over the dead boy's head. He moved the boy's brown hair aside to reveal the neck, where there was a purple abrasion similar to that upon FitzHerbert's neck, except that the mark ran straight around the neck and did not angle upward at the back. "Here, you can see. The boy was strangled."

Stephen turned FitzHerbert onto his stomach. The body was as flaccid as a bundle of rags, but he was a burly, well-muscled man and Gilbert's assistance proved to be necessary to get him stretched out. Stephen's objective was to look for other wounds or marks that might have contributed to the death. He examined the dead man's head to see if he had been struck there, but found nothing. The corpse was unblemished apart from that yellow waxy color on the back and chest and the purplish hue upon the buttocks and the backs of FitzHerbert's legs. Stephen, of course, was well familiar with these markings. A body which lay undisturbed for some time developed these different colors; the purple indicated the side that was or had been down.

The arrangement of these markings struck Stephen as curious. He stood up and fingered the length of rope dangling from the crossbeam. The end where it had been cut was at about the height of Gilbert's shoulder. Stephen held the end of the noose to the end of the rope. The noose itself was only three feet or so from the floor. This was very odd. FitzHerbert had died, apparently, with his buttocks only a few inches from the floor.

"You found him almost sitting," Stephen said.

"Yes," Curthose said. "I've never seen a man die like that. It made me wonder. Am I wrong? Is it important?"

"I don't know. Sometimes what you think is important at first turns out to mean nothing, and what you dismissed as insignificant turns out to settle the matter."

The examination of FitzHerbert completed, Stephen said, "Let's see to the boy."

Stephen and Gilbert performed the same diligent search for other wounds on the boy, but found none. They turned him over. Gilbert brushed the hair away from his face. He was a beautiful child with the face of an angel except for a broad jaw and overlarge mouth, yet it must have been sweet and sunny in life and was now composed as if he were asleep.

"What's his name?" Gilbert asked gazing down at the boy.

"Martin," Curthose said.

"Just Martin?" Gilbert said.

"He had no father. He lived with his mother and brood of siblings in a hovel on Grope Lane before his lordship plucked him from poverty. A band of beggars and thieves, they are, all the brats begat by different men. Sir Rogier found him begging outside a bathhouse."

"Indeed," Gilbert said as if to himself. "A bathhouse, was it?"

Stephen shot him a look to say no more about bathhouses. They were known with good reason as dens of prostitution, gambling and other forms of iniquity. The Church opposed them and occasionally went on campaigns to shut them down, but these efforts always met with failure, generally because the alderman of that area of the town received payments under the table to keep them open.

Stephen and Gilbert continued the examination. They found nothing untoward.

Stephen noticed a clay pitcher on the side table large enough to hold about a full gallon. It was almost empty. He sniffed the contents, which smelled of wine, but with an odd flowery fragrance that he had never detected in a wine before. But it was not unusual to flavor wine with herbs.

"Did his lordship like a tipple at bedtime?" Stephen asked.

"He often indulged himself," Curthose said.

"Quite a lot of indulgence for two," Gilbert said.

"Perhaps," Stephen said, "assuming it was filled to the top."

He carried the pitcher to the window so that the sunlight could reveal how far it had been filled. There was a stain about halfway up.

He rested the pitcher on the windowsill to consider whether this was important, and only then noticed the dark spots of something that had spilled upon it. And then as he leaned close to see what it might be, he saw below upon a pile of roofing slates left over from repairs what looked to be evidence that someone had poured something out the window. Wine perhaps? He could not imagine why anyone would waste wine in that way. He scraped one of the spots on the windowsill with the point of his dagger on the theory it was a blood spot and not wine. But it was not blood.

Stephen looked about for wine cups. One was on the long table. It was half full. The other was out of sight between a bedpost and the wall. It was a third full.

He strode out of the chamber and almost bumped into three servants clustered about the door so that they could overhear what was said and report it to the rest of the household.

He brushed by the servants and would have taken the stairway he had come up, but he spotted another to the right. "Where does that go?" Stephen asked Curthose.

"To the pantry and buttery," Curthose said.

"Is there a back entrance down there?"

"There is. Wait — can I have his lordship's body tended to now?"

Stephen glanced at Gilbert, who had just made it to the doorway. Gilbert nodded.

"Yes, and have a cup of wine fetched from the same barrel as last night," Stephen said and sped away down the back as fast as his bad foot would allow: he was missing half his left foot, which a Moor in Spain had cut off with an ax. Much of the time it did not bother him, but moving quickly could be difficult. He came down to the pantry and spotted the rear entrance. He went out the door which opened to a covered walkway leading to a kitchen a short distance away. He leaped over the rail bordering the walk and went around to the back of the hall. He was sniffing the spill on a roofing slate when Curthose caught up. The substance on the slate looked like a wine spill, dark red, but it had dried and there was no odor.

A servant bearing a wooden cup came around the corner. "You asked for a cup of wine, my lord?" He held it out to Curthose.

"Give it to Sir Stephen," Curthose said.

Before taking the cup, Stephen cut a mark on the stained roof tile in his hand with the tip of his dagger. Then he sniffed the cup. The wine lacked that odd fragrance. He poured the wine onto clean roof tile.

"See that this tile is not disturbed," Stephen ordered. "I'll be back when it has had time to dry."

"I don't understand," Curthose said.

"Neither do I, but it means something. I just don't know what yet. We've done all we can here. Please have the servants assemble in the hall."

Chapter 4

Stephen entertained his batch of servants at one end of the hall while Gilbert handled another batch at the other, with those awaiting questioning clustered about the hearth. It was a boring exercise but had to be done.

The only moment of interest came when the servants brought down FitzHerbert's body. There was silence in the hall, and those occupying the benches stood up and all watched respectfully as they bore out the body shrouded in a linen sheet.

Stephen and Gilbert, meanwhile, learned nothing: no one had seen or heard his lordship return from the city, for it had occurred after dark. Later there was a call for a pitcher of wine, and Martin had cracked the door to accept it.

"That sounds a bit unusual," Stephen remarked to the servant.

"It was," he said. "But I did not think anything of it at the time." He hesitated, and added guardedly, "His lordship and Martin often entertained themselves in his lordship's chambers during an evening."

"But normally, you just walked in with the pitcher?"

"Yes, upon knocking, of course. After his lordship got his pitcher we knew not to disturb him."

"Where did Martin sleep?"

The servant looked into a corner. "I'd prefer not to say. We do not speak of it."

"But it was not unusual to find him in his lordship's chamber in the morning?"

The servant stood up from his bench. "I'll say no more about our lordship. He was a good man, he treated us decently. I'll not be a party to the blackening of his name any further in death, nor give substance to any rumor about him."

"This is not about blackening his name."

"I said, I'll say no more." The servant turned away and marched toward the door to the pantry, giving Curthose a sharp look on the way out.

The interviewing interrupted the service of dinner, and about the time it should have come off, an elegant young woman dressed in a shimmering blue and yellow striped over gown with split sides and secured by a belt of silver links, her hair confined in a high round cap from which a silk overveil fell down her back, came out onto the top of the stairway overlooking the hall. She had remote eyes, high cheekbones and a small mouth pursed with impatience. This had to be Sir Rogier's widow, the Lady Isabel. A lesser woman almost equally well-gowned, obviously a maid from a prosperous gentry family, came out with her. Lady Isabel spoke to the maid who hurried down the steps and approached Curthose.

"Sir Geoffrey," the maid said, "her ladyship desires that those people not be admitted." She was as beautiful and striking as the Lady Isabel in her own way: pale skin, slightly freckled on the cheeks and nose, curls of reddish hair visible at the edge of her wimple, bright green eyes made for laughing but now full of determination. She caught Stephen staring and looked away with a jerk of the head.

"What people, Lady Madeline?" Curthose asked, perplexed.

"The mother of that boy," Madeline said, glancing toward the door. "They have just come into the yard. Her ladyship wishes that they be driven off at once."

Curthose sighed. "I am sure they have come for Martin's body. They have a right to that."

Madeline looked back to the stairs, where her ladyship was watching. Her ladyship nodded curtly. "They shall not come into the house."

"Very well, my lady," Curthose said. He turned to Stephen. "Can we release the boy's body?"

"I cannot see why not," Stephen said.

While Curthose ordered two servants to fetch the boy's body and another to halt the family in the yard, her ladyship called to Madeline, "Please see what has happened to dinner. Lady Aleusa and I cannot wait any longer."

"Yes, my lady," Madeline said and hurried through the doorway to the pantry. Her ladyship swung about, her skirts billowing, and stepped back through the doorway to the bedchambers.

"Things will be very different around here now," Curthose sighed as Stephen turned to the next servant to interview.

But before Stephen resumed the questioning, he asked Curthose, "Who is Lady Aleusa?"

"His lordship's mother."

Shortly, the two servants dispatched to fetch the corpse appeared at the top of the stairway. The body was swaddled in a linen sheet. They struggled down the stairs with it, one at each end, and carried the burden outside. Where you might expect the corpse to be greeted with wailing and lamentation, there was only silence. Then a cart creaked. Stephen glimpsed several boys and girls pulling a hand cart through the gate and turning toward town. A pair of feet that had come free of the sheet stuck into the air.

That should have been the end of it, but a woman with a frog-like face weathered and lined from hard use appeared at one of the windows. Gray hair straggled from beneath her wimple, one eyelid drooped as if in a squint, and when she spoke, there were several gaps where teeth should be.

"I want his wages!" the woman demanded.

"Go away, Peg," Curthose said. "This is not the time for it."

"And his effects! All those pretty clothes he got!"

"Do not make a scene," Curthose said. "Her ladyship will not stand for it."

"Her ladyship can —"

"You will not disrespect Lady Isabel!" Curthose thundered. "If you don't leave this moment, I will have you whipped out of the yard! We will square up tomorrow or the next day."

"You better not short change me!" Peg wagged a finger at him, not impressed with the threat, even though Stephen reckoned it was a real one. She marched away with the aid of a knobby stick, muttering things Stephen could not hear.

A train of servants appeared from the pantry bearing trays of food, which they carried upstairs. Many of the servants looked longingly at the food, for the questioning delayed their own meal, until at last Stephen and Gilbert finished and there was a flurry of activity, the setting up of tables and benches, and other servants brought out trays and trenchers for the household.

"Would you care to stay for dinner?" Curthose asked.

Stephen was about to demure. But Gilbert was assessing with an envious eye the mussel soup, the baked haddock and eel, leavened with boiled carrots and leeks, and the fresh white bread at the high table exuding the mouthwatering aroma of yeast.

"I would be glad to," Stephen said. "Thank you. Lady Isabel won't be coming down, I suppose."

"I doubt it," Curthose said, leading Stephen to a chair at the high table that was being put out for him. "She often takes her meals in her chamber when she is in residence."

"She and Sir Rogier did not get along?" Stephen asked as he settled into the chair and a servant pushed it forward for him, while Gilbert got a bench at the end, but at least it was at the high table where the fresh white bread was.

"He called her his brood mare," Curthose said. "To her face."

"I see," Stephen said, although he did not see. He could speculate, but he had learned the dangers of that, so he let silence reign to encourage Curthose to fill it and relieve his ignorance.

Curthose sighed. "It was his mother's idea, the marriage, I mean. Lady Aleusa is a formidable woman. Few people have the mettle to defy her, although Sir Rogier did a good job of it for years."

"How so?"

"By putting off marriage for so long. But in the end, he had no choice, really, if the line was to go on."

"Lady Isabel knew what he was?"

"From the start. Most people would never guess just to look at him. He hid it well, as one must do. But she was not fooled." Curthose shrugged. "But she did her duty, the poor girl. She delivered a son not two months ago. All of us were relieved at that, her most of all, I'm sure."

Stephen and Gilbert went out to the back garden after dinner to check on the roof tile doused with wine. Stephen placed the tile he had marked against the one on which he had poured the wine.

"Rather a match, I think," Gilbert said.

"Yes," Stephen said. He glanced up at the open window of FitzHerbert's chamber. "Someone likely poured out the contents of that pitcher. But why?"

"Bad wine, perhaps?"

"Would you pour it out? Wine's expensive. Most people just water it down."

"Well, I'm not filthy rich, like FitzHerbert. Nor are you."

"But some of my family is. And I know what they are likely to do. Or rather, I know what their stewards would do with a cask of bad wine: sell it or water it. And the wine we were given was from the same barrel. It was all right."

Gilbert scuffed the dirt with a toe. "You know, if it was the pitcher someone poured out, there wasn't much left in it."

"What?" Stephen asked.

"Look about. There was hardly enough poured out to fill a cup."

Curthose interrupted this conversation as he came around the corner of the house. His mouth opened to say something, but he in turn was interrupted by a call from the window above their heads.

"My lord!" a servant cried, leaning out. "The box! It has been opened!"

"Opened?" Curthose cried in reply.

He ran into the house.

"A strange box," Gilbert mused as he stretched to relieve an aching back unhappy with all the bending that had been required in examining the tiles. "How curious. I wonder what could be in it?"

"Money," Stephen said, following Curthose but at a more sedate pace due to the fact that his bad foot did not like running unless its life depended on it. "What else could it be to cause such distress?"

When Stephen reached FitzHerbert's bedchamber, Curthose was kneeing before the wardrobe peering into the box, an iron-bound chest chained to a leg of the wardrobe. Stephen had not noticed it before because it was out of sight within the wardrobe. The maid, Lady Madeline, and several servants were clustered about him, also transfixed.

"What was in the box?" Stephen asked Curthose, although his eyes were on Madeline.

"His lordship's traveling money," Curthose said. "Quite a lot of it. Fully five pounds of silver at the last counting. It's missing. Almost every penny."

"Reason enough for murder," Gilbert murmured.

"Indeed, if that was the object," Stephen said. "Did FitzHerbert always carry such a vast sum about?"

"He was planning a journey."

"Where, may I ask?" Gilbert said.

"To Wales, as if it's any business of yours," Curthose said.

"Whatever for?" Stephen asked. Although the war that had erupted during the winter had sputtered out, a trip to Wales was still a dangerous business. The land was full of freebooters and minor lords who supplemented their income robbing travelers.

Curthose hesitated to answer for he seemed to feel he had made a mistake in mentioning the endpoint of the journey, and Madeline spoke instead.

"He was an adherent of the reform party, as I am sure you know," Madeline said. "He was asked by none other than Lord Simon de Montfort to speak personally to Prince Llywellyn on his behalf."

"Say no more, my lady," Curthose said. "That is enough."

"I am not under your command, sir, with all due respect," Madeline said. But she said no more and went out.

"You were startled that the chest was open," Stephen said. "Why?"

"His lordship always kept it locked. But as you can see, the lock has been opened." Curthose pointed to a padlock beside the chest. He gazed toward the spot by the foot of the bed where FitzHerbert's body had lain. "I can see no reason for him to have opened the box."

"There was a key, then," Gilbert said.

"What of it?" Curthose asked.

"Where is it?"

Curthose's eyes wandered about the chamber. "I don't know. I don't recall seeing it."

"Where was it normally kept?"

"On a chain about his lordship's neck."

"I don't recall seeing any such chain when we examined him."

Curthose breathed heavily. "Nor do I remember seeing it."

"So where has it gone?" Gilbert mused. He wandered about the chamber, looking into all the corners, checked upon the table, and ruffled through the bedsheets. Then he got down on hands and knees and looked under the bed. "Ah, there it is. Stephen, could you lend a hand? I am afraid I cannot reach it."

"Robert," Curthose ordered one of the servants, "fetch the key."

"No," Stephen said, dropped to his belly beside Gilbert. "I'll do it."

He spotted the key on a delicate chain just over an arm's length from the edge of the bed board. The problem for Gilbert was the board was too low for him to fit beneath it, owing to his ample belly, but Stephen, with his lean frame, could crawl under.

"That is beneath you!" Curthose gasped.

"When it comes to examining the evidence, nothing is beneath me, I am afraid," Stephen said as he wormed under the bed. He grasped the chain and retreated. As he withdrew, he noticed something that escaped his attention before. By one of the bedposts, there was an indentation in the floorboard as if the post had originally lain there and a long scratch on the floor. The scratch was fresh. Jolted perhaps in a struggle? Stephen measured the scrape: it was as just short of the width of his hand, say, three or four inches. It put the bed out of alignment with the wall, a thing he had not registered earlier.

The chain and key in his palm, Stephen climbed to his feet. As he did so, he noticed something else. On the post nearest the window just above the mattress, one of the figures, that of an elephant, was damaged, missing its trunk and a tusk.

He ran a finger along the damaged part, but he had the key on his mind and he said, "It could not have got there by accident."

"I agree," Gilbert said, as they climbed to their feet. "So you think that his lordship might have taken it off and tossed it under the bed in a moment of passion?"

"I doubt you think so," Stephen said. "That would have required him to open the chest for no reason that any of us can think of, then toss the chain away, which I doubt he was in the habit of doing." He turned to Curthose. "What else might the chest have contained?"

"Leave us," Curthose ordered the servants. He shut the door after them and turned to Stephen and Gilbert. "You must not repeat this to anyone. There was a letter," he continued with some difficulty, the words halting. "His lordship was to deliver it to the prince."

"Do you know what was in the letter?" Stephen asked.

"No. His lordship did not speak of its contents. I only know that it was a matter of the utmost importance."

"And this letter . . . it's no longer here?" Stephen bent over the box. There was no letter in evidence.

"No. It's missing as well."

"Was it well known that Sir Rogier was going to Wales on behalf of Montfort?"

"No, it was the greatest secret. I only know because his lordship wanted me to accompany him with his household troops. I sent out word for them to assemble here two days hence."

"Yet others in the family seem to know."

Curthose sighed. "I am afraid his lordship was not as attentive to the need for discretion as he might have been."

"Whom might he have told?"

"Only his mother, as far as I know."

"So you think."

"Yes."

"If Lady Aleusa knew and the maid, then I suspect the entire household was informed."

"They knew only that he was going to Wales. I impressed upon her ladyship and Lady Madeline the importance of the need not to speak about the reason. When questions arose among the staff, I said his lordship intended a pilgrimage to Saint David's."

Stephen nodded. Everyone knew of Saint David's, a great cathedral on the far west coast of Wales. People often made pilgrimages there. "A good enough excuse. Gilbert, is there anything more we can accomplish here?"

"I don't think so, other than having an accounting of the contents of the chest."

"I'll have that done," Curthose said.

Stephen paused in the hallway. He stepped to the door to Lady Isabel's chamber and knocked. The voices speaking within the chamber stopped at the knock, but no one came to answer the door, nor was there any call to enter. Stephen knocked again. Lady Madeline cracked the door. She had changed out of her gown and wore the white linen shift that went under the over gown. One thing marred her perfection, he now noticed, small stains on the fabric of her shift at the chest.

"Yes?" she inquired.

"I'd like to speak to Lady Isabel," Stephen said.

"She is not feeling well. Something she ate did not agree with her."

"What about Lady Aleusa? Is she here also?"

"She is not feeling well either."

"Then I'll talk to you."

"I have nothing to say."

"Did you hear anything or see anything out of the ordinary last evening?"

"Good day, sir."

Madeline shut the door.

Chapter 5

"A secret missive to the Prince of Wales," Gilbert said as they walked back to the city. "Is that worth killing for?"

"Could be, I suppose," Stephen said, head down, hands clasped behind his back as they walked back toward the city. "I don't know."

"If this matter is about the letter, it could put us in great danger. Who else would be responsible but someone from the King's faction? You have enemies enough already without making more of them."

"But we don't know that to be true yet. Are you saying we should give up?"

"Something to think about."

"Maybe later, when we know more."

"Having wasted our time to no profit. Nothing good is going to come from this, I'm sure of it."

They crossed the wooden bridge spanning the town ditch at Wydemarsh Gate. It was late afternoon and a succession of one-horse carts, pack horses, and hand carts coming out of town forced them to keep to the side of the road.

A couple of bored gate wardens lounged against the stone walls beneath the gate.

"Did either of you have the first watch last night?" Stephen asked.

"Not me," one said.

"Me neither," said the other. "That would be Nick."

"Nick?"

"Yeah, Nick."

"Just Nick?" Stephen asked, hoping for a last name, although not everyone had one.

"That's what we call him."

"Is he upstairs?" Many gate wards lived in the towers they were assigned to.

"Nah."

"Do know where he is?"

"Hey, you that fellow, Attebrook? The coroner from Ludlow?"

"I was the coroner from Ludlow. I've been replaced."

"Sorry about that. You were out at the FitzHerbert place, weren't you, sir?"

"I was."

"Is it true that the old man, I mean Sir Rogier, killed the boy and then hanged himself?"

"That's been suggested," Stephen said.

"You don't believe it?"

"It's too early to believe anything."

The guard who had done most of the talking shook his head. "Sir Rogier may have been a bit *odd,* you know, but he was a decent sort. Never rude or nasty to us, not like some of the snooty-nosed are, begging your pardon, sir. Nick says he always tipped well when he left the city."

"Sir Rogier had a habit of leaving town after curfew?"

"He weren't the only one, as you probably know yourself, but yes."

"Any idea what Sir Rogier was doing in the town so late?" Stephen asked.

"You'll have to ask Nick that," the talkative guard said.

"He never let on?"

"Not a peep."

"So, where is Nick?"

"He's got a house on Grope Lane. You might find him there. Do you know where that is, sir?"

"I'm familiar with Grope Lane."

"Why are you asking, sir? Is there some doubt about what happened to Sir Rogier?"

"No, I am just tying up some loose ends."

"Ah, something to do with his secret life, eh, sir?"

"Thanks, boys, and good day."

"Well, Grope Lane," Gilbert said. "At last I shall have the opportunity to see our local Sodom and Gomorrah."

"Gilbert," Stephen said, astonished. "I had not taken you for a lascivious man."

"I am not. But all my life I have heard of this place. At last, in my autumn years, I'll have the chance to see it."

Stephen strode on a bit down Wydemarsh Street toward the second marketplace where the high cross stood, which was visible in the distance. "Be prepared to be disappointed. It isn't much. Just a collection of shady inns and taverns overrun with gamblers, whores, and cutpurses. You've seen the like in London only on a grander scale."

"Oh. Well, then, you don't have to worry about protecting me from vice there, since I was able to resist London."

"No one gave you the chance to indulge in London. We were too busy. But if you insist, I will turn my back so that I don't have to witness your fall from grace and then have to lie about it to Edith."

"I am not contemplating any fall from grace, such as I enjoy. It's a mere professional interest. Harry will want to know, surely."

"Ah, it's for Harry. How thoughtful."

They turned the corner. Ahead was the guild hall, where the town clerks could observe activities in the market and catch those who had not paid their tolls, and over top of it the spire of Saint Peter's Church could be seen. Coken Row was a pretty sight off to the left of the guildhall, a narrow lane of timber-and-whitewashed houses, which the residents were required to keep looking bright and clean as this was part of the city market, and Stephen would have admired it more if it had not been for another sight.

Coming his way with a grim, yet satisfied expression on his face that filled Stephen with foreboding, was Percival FitzAllan. A squad of halberd-armed deputies marched behind him.

"There you are!" FitzAllan said with relish as he and Stephen met. FitzAllan waved a hand. "Take him!"

The deputies rushed around FitzAllan and surrounded Stephen. Gilbert stumbled backward, pushed out of the way. The deputies seized Stephen by the arms.

"What is this?" Stephen demanded.

"You are under arrest for the murder of William Attebrook," FitzAllan declared.

Chapter 6

FitzAllan's presence frightened Gilbert by itself, but to have the sheriff level an accusation of murder filled him with terror. And with good reason. Gilbert had been there when William Attebrook died boarding a Portuguese slave ship, and if Stephen was accused of causing that death, there was plenty of room to include Gilbert in the indictment if FitzAllan felt like it.

FitzAllan was too busy savoring his satisfaction at Stephen's arrest to notice that Gilbert was here. This enabled Gilbert to edge behind a cart filled with rubbish collected from the streets. The stench was choking. Gilbert gasped and put the end of his sleeve over his mouth. He bent down as if to tie his shoe, which took him out of sight of the sheriff and the deputies.

"Murder, is it?" Stephen asked. "Who brings this charge?"

"Sir William's widow," FitzAllan said.

"What does Elysande know of such things? She wasn't there when William died."

"She has a witness, one who *was* there."

"That would be Herb, I imagine. If he said that he lies." Herb was a servant at Hafton Manor, which Stephen inherited upon William's death. Herb had been there when William died in the attack on the Portuguese ship. But it had not been murder. William had been first up the ladder to the ship's deck and had been knocked off, disappearing into the dark Thames before anyone could catch him.

"It is what he said that counts, not whether it is the truth. Bring him!" FitzAllan marched toward the castle.

"I have a right to offer surety to ensure my answer to this charge!" Stephen said.

"Going lawyer on me, eh?" FitzAllan said. "I'll not debate trivial technicalities with you. You'll rot in gaol until the King's justice has time for you."

"It could be months before he comes here again!"

FitzAllan chuckled. "I am sure that's true. How unfortunate."

"You have no right to hold me, especially when I offer surety."

"Rights? You have only the rights I give you. I'm the sheriff. I'm the law in this county. It's my word that counts. Come, boys, let us not tarry!"

Every castle has its gaol. They varied according to the taste and needs of the constable. Some were former pig sties; others were mere stalls in barns. Still others were holes in the ground covered with boards, which had a habit of filling with water when it rained, often drowning the guests.

Hereford's gaol was more elaborate than these. It lay in the center of the dirt floor of the basement of the right hand gate tower, marked by planks set into the dirt with a trap door in the middle. At least, having benefit of a roof, it was not likely to fill with rain water.

The deputies threw up the trap door and pushed Stephen into the dark space beneath.

Stephen expected a long fall, but the gaol pit proved to be shallow: only four feet or so, to a stone floor.

The deputies tossed in a bucket which struck Stephen's shoulder.

"Mind you shit in that," one of the deputies instructed. "Don't want to stink up the place more than we have to. The constable likes his castle kept clean."

They dropped the trap door and slammed the bolt.

Stephen sat down and examined his new lodgings. There was enough light through cracks in the boards above his head to see after his eyes had time to adjust. He was in a circular pit walled in stone. He might be able to dig his way out, but it would take time and lots of effort. But he had time, likely plenty of it.

Using his belt buckle, he began scraping at the mortar between the cracks in two stones.

At the same moment that FitzAllan and the deputies marched off toward the castle, the workers manning the rubbish cart came away from the window of a nearby tavern where they had been enjoying a pitcher of ale, collected the cart and drew it off, leaving Gilbert crouched in the street. Gilbert looked about for other places to hide in case the officers happened to glance back. There was nothing close but a big stone trough used for public pissing, and Gilbert would have had to lie down behind it to avoid being seen. This would not do.

But the officers marched with such energy and authority that Gilbert quickly apprehended that no one would look back. He rose to his feet. As immediate danger withdrew, the panic welling in his mind subsided. What to do now?

His first thought was to flee up Wydemarsh Street and keep going until he reached home. He even turned in that direction. Then he stopped. If Elysande Attebrook was going to accuse Stephen, she'd have cast a wide net and named everyone involved, which necessarily included him. Thus, he reasoned, if he had not been arrested now, he had not been accused, and if he had not been accused now, he probably would not be. She was after Hafton Manor, and to get it she needed only to bring Stephen down. If Gilbert came into it, it would be as a witness, with the rack, hot irons, the smokebox, and thumbscrews to encourage favorable testimony.

Moreover, if he ran, he'd leave behind valuable property at the castle: the least of which was his spare clothing, a saddle and tack, Stephen's horse, and his mule. Property was hard to come by, and a man couldn't simply cast it away. His wife, Edith, would have his ear off before she sent him into hiding, and if he feared anyone's rage, it was hers.

So, with much trepidation and fretting, Gilbert followed FitzAllan's entourage back to the castle.

The main gate opened upon a lane between a row of houses on a street aptly named Castle Street. The gate sat across a wooden bridge over a water-filled moat, deeply recessed in two drum-shaped towers that were so tall it was a wonder they were not lost in low clouds. The walls of the castle, which sat on high earthen embankments, were made of white-plastered stone, the same as the towers, and at least twenty, perhaps even thirty feet tall, the whole a testimony to the power and wealth of the man who had built it, the King of England.

Gilbert drew a deep breath, crossed the bridge and went under the gate passage. Just any old body was not allowed in, and Gilbert expected to be challenged for an explanation for his right of entry. But one of the gate wardens nodded, a sign of recognition. And Gilbert got through.

As he left the gate's massive, iron-studded doors in his wake, he saw FitzAllan and several of the deputies heading off through the tents of people who had come for the assembly toward the great hall on the other side of the bailey. The door to the ground floor of the northern tower was open and Gilbert heard voices within, one of them Stephen's. This must be the gaol.

"Good," he said to himself. "All I have to do is pick the lock and we can both be away." But of course that was not going to happen. He knew nothing about the picking of locks and the manner of being away — escaping from a castle sealed for the night — was beyond his talents.

A familiar voice murmured in his ear, "Come away, Gilbert. Someone will notice your interest."

Gilbert nearly jumped out of his coat. "Walter! You gave me such a shock!"

Walter, one of Lady Margaret de Thottenham's retainers, a thick-set soldierly man with a rugged face like a piece of wind-weathered rock, grasped his sleeve and led him away through the tents some distance before they came upon a campfire with benches around it. Walter sat on one of the benches and drew Gilbert down beside him.

"What am I to do, Walter?" Gilbert lamented. "What am I to do? I was there! I saw it all!"

"The first thing you do is keep your voice down. The second thing you do is not mention a word of that death or your part in it to anyone."

"That is easy on my part, but there are others who know. Herbert of Hafton Manor, for instance." Gilbert had a fuzzy recollection of having heard Herb's name mentioned at the time of Sir Stephen's arrest.

"Yes, Herb, we heard about him. He's the one giving evidence against Sir Stephen. But he hasn't mentioned you."

"He's here?" Gilbert asked, voice rising despite his efforts to keep it under control.

"Yes, and a prisoner himself. And likely to remain so."

"Oh, dear! Oh, dear!"

"I don't think he's giving his testimony voluntarily, if you know what I mean." Walter cocked an eye at Gilbert as if to say, you could be in the same boat if word got out.

"I have thought of that already. Oh, yes!" Gilbert's panting began to slacken, though. He closed his eyes and breathed deeply. He began to feel calmer, but only just. "What now?"

"Collect your things and Sir Stephen's. There is an inn on the Wydemarsh Road without the gate, the Trumpet, it's called. Wait there until you hear from me."

The work went on until it was too dark to see, pausing now and then when Stephen heard voices above, people who might be close enough to detect the scraping. He hoped for someone to come with a crust of moldy bread and brackish water, but night fell without any such courtesy.

He sat with his back to a wall, for the floor stones were hard and unforgiving, not conducive to sleep. Plans for revenge against Elysande bumbled through his head, but they were nothing more than entertainment. He would realize none of them. He hoped Gilbert had got away. But even if he had, Gilbert would be dragged into the affair and ruined if not killed eventually. Gilbert was the only other witness, and he could not be allowed to talk. Stephen drifted off to sleep at last.

The day brought no more food or water than the night had done, and Stephen was so thirsty by the end of it that he considered drinking his own piss. He had never done this himself, but he remembered a story from a friend in Spain about an acquaintance who had fallen from his horse in the arid lands and broken a leg, dying when he could no longer resist the urge to drink his urine. It was a bad thing. Or so he had been told.

At nightfall, he heard the loud sounds of merriment above in what had to be the guardroom, where the tower wardens ate and slept so the main gate would never be undefended. As time went on, the volume of voices and laughter increased, an indication that they were getting very drunk.

Stephen expected the amusements to carry on late into the night, but after about an hour, things settled down. He supposed that the gate captain had put a squash on the merriment, for someone of the company had to remain at least relatively sober if duty was to be done.

Then the bolt rattled and the trap door drew up.

"Good God!" a familiar voice whispered. "What a fucking stink! Come on! What are you waiting for? Me to come in and carry your sorry arse out?"

"Hello, Walter," Stephen said as he lifted himself through the door and stood up. "I am surprised to see you."

"This is the last time I spring you from gaol," said Walter, carefully lowering the door and slipping the bolt into place. He glanced up at the floor above where the drinking had taken place. "It's too dangerous a pastime. Come on, before any of them wake up."

The door to the tower basement opened into the bailey. They slipped out and stood quietly for a moment, searching for the location of the watch. Soft padding and scraping in the distance on either side enabled them to locate the wardens walking the wall.

When the watch seemed to be heading away, Walter set off across the bailey, his arm over Stephen's shoulders as if they had consumed a bit more than was prudent.

The last time Stephen had seen the bailey, it had been filled with the tents of those who had come for the assembly, but many of them were gone now. So they were able to make their way straight across without meeting anyone.

Walter's objective was the great barn on the wall along the river. The door was open a crack and they slipped inside. Above Stephen's head in the loft, a woman laughed softly and a man's voice murmured in response. There was some rustling to the left as well. The lowest servants at a castle often slept in the barn, so he was not surprised to find people here, but he had no idea why Walter had led him here.

Walter handed Stephen a clay pot which he had carried in a cloth satchel. Stephen drank from it: it was cool, clean water. He gulped the entire contents. He handed Walter the pot and received a large chunk of cheese, which Stephen made disappear with only a few ravenous bites.

"You could try chewing with a bit less noise, sir," Walter whispered.

"Sorry. Old habit when I'm starving."

Walter took Stephen's arm and steered him along the wall until they came to an unhitched cart. "There is a barrel waiting for you. Make yourself comfortable in it."

"Now?" Stephen asked.

"Yes. You don't want to chance being discovered in the morning if you sleep on the ground."

"I hope it is a comfortable barrel," Stephen said, setting a foot on the deck of the cart while Walter steadied it.

"I'm sorry, we didn't have the time to get one of those," Walter said as he pressed Stephen's head down and settled the barrel's top into place. "Sleep tight."

It was impossible, of course, to sleep in the barrel. It wasn't long before it grew uncomfortable, his knees drawn up to his chin, and then painful. Stephen almost wished for the gaol pit. At least he could stretch out there. But he endured it, as he had to do. There was no other choice.

After many hours of this torment, Stephen heard others stirring in the barn. Birds chirped and a cock crowed nearby, officially signaling the arrival of the dawn.

People went out to the privy and to start the day's work, while others came in to fetch supplies for the kitchen.

After another agonizing hour, Stephen felt the cart tilt, which caused his heart to leap as he imagined the barrel tumbling off until he realized that someone was hitching a horse to it.

The cart started forward with a jolt and left the barn. It made jolting progress across the bailey and continued jolting along for a long time, years probably.

At last, the jolting stopped and someone rapped on the lid of the barrel.

"Wake up, dearie," a woman said. "We're here."

"It's impossible to sleep the way you drive that cart." Stephen lifted the lid to find out where here was. It was the inside of another barn, although much smaller than the one in the castle.

A young woman dressed in a churl's brown gown and cloak, which was frayed at the cuffs and hems from long use, stood above him.

"Don't like me driving, eh? I'm sure you'd have preferred to walk then. Come on, dearie," she said. "You can't spend all day in there. I've got deliveries to make."

"Right, sorry," Stephen said, standing with some difficulty. "Do I owe you anything for the ride?"

"That's already taken care off. Now hurry, before someone comes in."

"Doing my best."

He managed to crawl out of the barrel unaided and got down from the cart with more difficulty. The woman hopped down and guided the horse and cart out of the barn.

Walter was leaning against a support beam. He came away from it. "This way, sir."

They emerged into a yard of what had to be an inn. Walter climbed the back stairs to the first floor. He stopped at the door to one of the chambers and held it open for Stephen, who went inside.

Walter remained outside and shut the door.

Margaret de Thottenham was seated on a stool by the window overlooking the street. She was a vision as always, made even more so by the golden morning light streaming through the window. There was no woman alive who had a face so gentle and sweet and innocent, so inspiring of a man's need to protect her, those blue eyes so beseeching and often full of amusement, her neck and arms graceful and swanlike. Yet there was also no other woman Stephen knew who was so full of iron, so strong and capable of deception. She settled the book she had been reading on her lap.

"Oh, Stephen," she said in her musical voice, "Percival hates you so. I had no idea how much."

"Well, you're partly the cause of that," Stephen said.

She dipped her magnificent head in acknowledgement that his statement was partly true. "He was going to let you die in that pit. It would have settled so many issues, the least of which is Elysande's claim."

"And how is Elysande? I assume you've seen her."

"I was there when she appealed to Percival about the murder of her husband. I assume that is a lie."

"Of course, it is a lie."

"What really happened?"

"That is a tale for another day. What do you want from me this time?"

"Must we talk business now? It has been a long time since we've seen each other. We have a lot of catching up to do." She gestured toward a small table where there was a pitcher and wash bowl. "Do get cleaned up. Gaols are such messy places. I've brought you some new clothes as well. Not what you're used to, but in the current circumstances, I think you need something different."

With that, Margaret stepped away from the window and reached behind her back to undo the stays of her gown. She pulled it over her head and stood before him in only her shift, which quickly followed the gown to the floor. She was naked.

Stephen stared, transfixed at the sight, as she settled onto the bed.

"Make haste, Stephen," she said. "It's getting late. There is a great deal to do and we do not have much time."

Chapter 7

Stephen would have liked to lie in bed and he almost dozed off, but Margaret rose and gathered her shift and gown. She pulled them over her head one at a time and said, "Help with the stays, will you?"

"No pillow talk, then?" Stephen asked, rising to do as he was bid.

"I am afraid not, as much as I would like to."

"I thought that was part of my reward."

"You got your reward when Walter sprang you from gaol."

"What are you doing with FitzAllan?" The question came out more sharply than Stephen had intended, and he regretted asking it. It made him sound like a jealous fool.

Margaret smiled slightly. "That is not your concern." But she paused, then said, "It was Nigel's idea. He doesn't trust FitzAllan. He thinks FitzAllan will change his allegiance again. I'm to keep an eye on him and see if he is trying to persuade others to do the same. Now, tell me. What did you learn at FitzHerbert's house? Was it really suicide?"

"I don't think so. It seems like a murder to me, but there is no real proof. He was on a mission for Montfort to the prince of Wales. It seems unlikely that such a man would kill himself."

"He was a bit frail emotionally, but I agree with you." The stays secured, Margaret faced Stephen. "Was anything missing from his possessions?"

"Why do you ask that odd question?"

"Was there a letter not found where it was supposed to be?"

"I was told by the steward that a letter seemed to be missing. What do you know about that?"

"FitzHerbert confided in me after he arrived that he had an important letter. It contained our lord's proposed terms to the prince."

"Sounds important."

"Of course, it is important — supremely important." Margaret paced to the window and swung back. "I need you to get that letter from whoever stole it, before it falls into the hands of the King's supporters."

"Margaret, you know whose side I am on."

"You owe me a favor, Stephen." She crossed the room and laid her hands on his chest. "Come join us, Stephen! Your fortune can be made with us, not with the King! You are nothing but a little man to him and Edward, to be used as they will, and tossed aside afterward. We can make you great. I can make you great."

"Next you'll say that you'll find a way to get me a pardon from this murder business."

Margaret smiled. "That shouldn't be hard. Finding that letter will be worth a pardon from someone."

Stephen looked to a stool in the corner, where a folded brown shirt, green stockings, and battered red felt hat lay. He fetched them and put them on. They were a peasant's simple clothes, but at least there was a good belt with a quality dagger hanging from it. It was good to have that dagger at his hip. He always felt naked without one.

"I can't promise you that I will pursue this letter. It may be of interest to me, but only insofar as it has anything to do with FitzHerbert's death."

"You are pigheaded. Men and their honor." She smiled. "If you find the letter, you will give it to me?"

"We will have to see."

He could tell she was suppressing the urge to stamp her foot.

"All right then," Margaret said. "No promises. Do you have a place of refuge in town?"

"There's a house in Jews Street. It belongs to a man named Theo Tennet."

"I imagine that you'll want Gilbert's help. I shall direct him there, then. And I imagine you could use expense money." Margaret fetched a purse from her leather bag and held it out to Stephen.

"You can't buy me this way."

"I'm not trying to. But perhaps you might, at some point, feel grateful for my help and be willing to do me a turn in repayment."

"My lady." Stephen took the money. He regretted it, but put it in his belt pouch nonetheless. Perhaps it was his desperation that made him weak. He touched the edge of his hat as a peasant would do.

And he went out.

Stephen left the door open. Walter came in and shut it. Margaret was looking out the window and did not turn at his entrance.

"He won't give you the letter if he finds it, will he, my lady," Walter said.

"No," Margaret said, her back to him so he could not see her face. "He won't."

"Did you expect him to?"

"No, not at all. But now he knows how important it is and what might be done with it."

"Do you think that was wise?"

"Of course, it wasn't wise. It was the most foolish thing I've ever done."

She swept by Walter toward the stairway to the ground floor. "Come," she said, "we must get some shopping done before we go back to the castle. Otherwise, FitzAllan might suspect something is up."

Chapter 8

Stephen emerged into the street. He paused to get his bearings. The inn, under the sign of a black lion, was three houses down from the Wye Bridge, a good place for an inn. He chuckled humorlessly that such a thought entered his head. He had been around Gilbert too long.

He felt his courage ebbing. His bold front to Margaret had been a charade. The truth was, he was exhausted, frightened and full of doubt. He was an outlaw now. The smart thing was to run for it, leave the country. But he could not move in that direction, or any other.

He felt eyes on him, although they belonged to none of the people in the street, who hurried by consumed by their own affairs. He was nothing to them, just another blockage that had to be stepped around.

He glanced at the window overhead. Margaret was looking down at him. He felt another pang of desire for her. He wished she felt the same. But she was all about getting what she wanted. He knew this. I am a fool, he thought.

He hurried up the street and soon passed out of her sight.

Stephen's feet led him to the end of Bridge Street, where Saint Nicholas' Church, a magnificent stone edifice sat like an island in the middle of the street. His feet knew to turn left toward Plow Lane, a narrower, lesser passage than Wrotethale and Brode Streets to the right, where wandering bailiffs were likely to be found who might recognize him. The broad brim of his felt hat, which he pulled low, gave him no comfort it would hide him from close inspection.

Plow Lane ran north and ended at Behynderthewall Lane. This forced Stephen's feet to make another decision: right or left? The feet went right, although he looked yearningly to the left, for in that direction lay Eign Gate and beyond the countryside.

At the top of Brode Street a lane opened in the rank of houses. It was little more than an alley, hardly wide enough for two men to pass without bumping into each other. His feet turned down the alley, which deposited him at All Saints

Church by the foot of Wydemarsh Street, where the marketplace began and ran to the east toward Saint Peter's Church.

Stephen hesitated here, worried about the possibility of town bailiffs, for the guildhall lay only a short distance away to the right. Who knew who might be watching from its windows.

Mouth dry, Stephen hurried into Wydemarsh Street. It wasn't far now to the gate and relative freedom. He was breathing hard.

But then Malieres Street gaped to the right and his feet rushed down it. Halfway, it changed its name to Jews Street, on account of the Jews who had once lived here. They were long gone now, but the name remained.

At last he reached a modest timber and wattle house. A blonde woman, her hair braided as befitted a married woman and stuffed under her wimple with only a few strands showing, was sweeping off the porch of the house. Her face had the same strong jaw with a crease on the chin sported by a friend of his named Harry, formerly known as Harry the beggar, but now a man of means and a career in woodcarving. Once or twice Stephen had even recently heard him referred to as Harry the Carver, although as far as he knew nobody had yet called Harry that to his face. Memories were long in Ludlow and it was likely to be some time before Harry's troubled and lowly past was forgotten.

Stephen wanted to speak to her but his voice had stopped working.

The woman glanced up at him standing at her stoop. Her lips started to form words, probably, what the hell you staring at? Or, what do you want?

But recognition dawned in her pretty blue eyes and her mouth formed a startled O.

Then she grasped Stephen's shirt front and pulled him into the house.

"What in God's name are you doing here?" the woman exclaimed as she shut the door and threw down the bar.

"Looking for a place to hide," Stephen managed.

"And your first thought was of us. I'm flattered."

The first thing Sarah Tennet did after she deposited Stephen on a bench in the hall was summon her boys, who had been playing in a pile of dirt in the back yard.

She lined the boys up before Stephen and said, "You remember Sir Stephen?"

The oldest boy, Mike, and the second one, Harry, who were eight and six, nodded, their brown hair shaking about their heads. The youngest, Ralph, who was two, nodded, too, although it seemed doubtful he was doing more than copying his elders.

"Sure do!" Mike said. "Why are you dressed funny?"

"Well," Sarah said, "you'll not say a word that he's back. If you do, I'll tan the hide off you." To emphasize her seriousness, Sarah had armed herself with a switch which she snapped at the boys' back legs, not hard but enough to get their attention.

"You were in gaol, weren't you?" Mike asked. "Dad said so."

"And you escaped," Harry said with wonder. "How'd you manage that?"

"Nobody's supposed to know," Stephen said. "That's what you've got to keep quiet about. Can you do it?"

"Sure!" both boys said.

"I hope so," Sarah said. "By cause if anyone finds out he's here, they'll have the skin off your dad's back. Not to mention mine. You don't want to be orphans, do you? Think about all the bad things that happen to them."

This brought serious expressions to the boys' faces more readily than the prospect of a switching.

"You can count on us," Mike declared.

"All right, then. You go play. But mind you, not a word."

Stephen buried his face in his palms. "Do you think they'll obey?"

Sarah shrugged. "They've kept quiet about their dad's work."

"He's back at it?" Stephen was surprised to hear this. Sarah's husband, Theo, had been a burglar, supposedly reformed and law abiding now except for one job Stephen and Theo had pulled off together.

"He never really quit. It's one way we make ends meet when things get tight." Her face grew angry. "Like that horse we got somehow. I can't imagine how Theo came by that."

Stephen had given Theo a horse as payment for helping him recover a valuable object from the depths of Hereford castle. He said, "I hope it brought enough that you don't have to worry about money for a while."

"There is that. He hasn't been in any mischief since that business of yours. He thinks we don't know, but we do." She sat on the bench opposite Stephen, and put down a half round of cheese and a half loaf of bread. "I can't help but worry, though. You never know what the future holds."

"Looks like war."

"We'll stay out of it and let the rich people kill each other, and the poor fools who follow them." She reached for the ale pitcher and refilled Stephen's cup. "Harry sent me a letter."

Stephen was shocked. "He did?"

"Paid to have it delivered himself. He told me how you set him up in the woodcarving business. I want to thank you for what you've done for him. After his accident, when he lost his legs, I thought he was done for. It's the only reason I've allowed you in the house."

"I'll try not to bring doom upon your head."

"See that you don't."

Stephen lifted his head from the table.

"Hey, sleepy-head," Sarah said from the back doorway, where she was carding wool. "Feeling better?"

"Yes," Stephen said. "A lot, actually." He could not remember putting his head down to sleep. The last thing he recalled was resting his face in his hands while trying to think of what to do next. Now several hours had passed. Gilbert had not yet come, and it was getting late if he planned to question Nick the gate warden.

He stood up, and headed toward the front door.

"You're leaving?" Sarah asked.

"Yes."

"Will you be back?"

"When I've finished my business."

"Go out the back. There's an alley across the yards that opens into Bye Street. Use that when you return."

The alley Sarah had spoken of was a narrow slit of a thing barely wide enough for a grown man to fit through. The houses bordering the alley were large and well kept, rising three stories above the ground, the garden on the left quite large and elaborate, having not only cabbage, peas, and onions, but also a profusion of herbs.

The alley opened onto Bye Street about fifty or sixty yards from Bye Gate. As Stephen looked about to get his bearings, the reason for the herb garden became apparent. An apothecary's sign loomed above his head to the left, and a woman was at the front window asking after something that would help her sleep.

Stephen went around the woman and her maid toward Bye Gate. The maid cast him a disdainful glance as he pulled the brim of his felt hat down so that the guards at the gate would not get a good look at his face. Although there was no reason to suppose he would be recognized by anyone, he felt as though he had a sign pinned to his back announcing his identity.

However, he got around the corner into Old Street without anyone seeing that sign and walked up to Grope Lane, which was about a hundred-fifty yards from the gate.

He asked the first person he met in Grope Lane, a woman carrying a bundle of laundry wrapped in a sheet on her back, where Nick the gate ward lived.

"What could ya possibly want him for?" the woman asked.

"I owe him money," Stephen said.

The woman looked him up and down as though she didn't believe this. "You'll find him fifth house from the wall on the right."

Grope Street was known for its whores, taverns and gambling dens, so there was bound to be a bailiff or two about to put a stop to any fights or disturbances that broke out. It was early, and the real drinking and gambling didn't commence until the patrons got off work at the end of the day. Still, a bailiff emerged from a tavern with four tables set out in the street. The bailiff goosed a whore sitting at a table, identifiable by her yellow wimple. She slapped the offending hand away, with a sharp, "Off with ya, ya pocksy lout!"

"I'll see ya tonight, Ellie," the bailiff leered.

"Be sure you bring a penny. No more free stuff for you!"

The bailiff turned away from Ellie, gave Stephen the up-and-down, assessing his capacity for trouble, then strolled off toward Bye Street. Stephen sighed with relief at not being recognized.

At that moment, the woman Peg whom Stephen had seen in the yard of the FitzHerbert house emerged from a house across from the tavern. She strode across the street to Ellie without the help of her knobby stick, and plopped onto the bench. When he had last seen her in the yard of FitzHerbert's house, she had worn a plain brown gown that was soiled and ragged at the hem, patched here and there, a natty wimple and rumpled apron. Peg's attire today was far different: something a woman of the gentry might wear, a round little hat with a spotlessly clean and white silk veil that wrapped around her face and concealed her wrinkled neck, a flowing overgown that was embroidered with hunt scenes, and a long sleeved undergown of red silk. It all must have cost a pretty penny.

"Since you've got no business going, I want you to get Martin's stuff from those bastards, and his wages," Peg said, rubbing her drooping eye.

"All right, Ma," Ellie said. But she did not move.

"Now!" Peg commanded.

Ellie stood up. "What if they don't give 'em to me?"

"Then you don't leave until that fucker Curthose gives you satisfaction. I want what's owed. We need it. Things are going to be tight again without what he brought in."

"All right, all right!" Ellie waved a hand as she walked away toward Bye Street. "Get off my back!"

"I'll show you what it's like to be on your back!" Peg cried and dashed after Ellie, the knobby stick raised. Peg did not get close, though, because Ellie took off running, beat her to the corner, and passed out of sight.

Peg came back, twirling her stick.

She gave Stephen the eye as she returned to the bench. "What you looking at, arsehole?"

"Nothing," he said.

"Then get your arse out of here," Peg snapped. She leaned back and called over her shoulder. "Ale! I need a fucking ale!"

People were looking at Stephen now, so he hurried down Grope Lane. The lane met the wall and ran along it out of sight, but it wasn't hard to spot the fifth house on the right. It had a tavern on the ground floor, but there were stairs just inside the front door leading up to the first floor. Stephen climbed the stairs and rapped on the door.

He heard a small girl's voice behind the door, then it opened. A woman's freckled face showed in the gap.

"Who is it, Mum?" asked the little girl who was out of sight.

"What do you want?" the woman demanded.

"Does Nick the gate ward live here?" Stephen asked.

"What business is it of yours whether he does or not?"

"I just wanted to ask a question."

"Huh." The woman looked down the stairs to see if anyone else was there. "Wait a moment." She shut the door.

A long time passed before the door opened again. This time a stocky man much shorter and broader than Stephen stood in the gap. He held a long, slim dagger in his stubby fingers. He also looked down the stairs to see if Stephen was alone.

"You Nick?" Stephen asked.

"What if I am? What do you want?"

"Geoffrey Curthose asked me to make an inquiry into the days before his lordship's death."

"You don't look the sort that Curthose would ask to clean a privy."

"He doesn't want to spend much on it."

"No wonder. He's got to fall back on his little manor now that he's been discharged."

This was news to Stephen but he shrugged as if he already knew it.

"So what's this got to do with me?" Nick asked.

"I'm told you were on the gate when he and Martin came through the night they died."

Nick leaned against the door jamb and began to pick his fingernails with the tip of the dagger. "I was."

"You remember it?"

"Sure. There wasn't much to it. They came through. Sir Rogier tipped me well, as he always did, and that was that."

"There wasn't anything unusual? Nothing out of the ordinary?"

"They did have another fellow with them, but that wasn't unusual either."

"Did you know this fellow?"

Nick shook his head, frowning at the effort to remember. "No, can't say that I got a look at him. He had his hood up."

"Just the one fellow?"

"Just the one. I figured he was another of the boys FitzHerbert was always bringing home. They come through after dark so they wouldn't be noticed. That's why he tipped so well — he was more decent than most, but I'm sure it was so that I'd keep me lips shut. Now that he's dead, I guess it doesn't matter so much. It wasn't a great secret what kind of man he was. And now with the hanging, everybody knows."

"FitzHerbert was in the habit of bringing other boys to his house? Even though he had Martin?"

"Yeah, he liked his threesome."

"Squinty Peg, would that be Martin's mum?"

"She is, or was." Nick scratched an itch in his privates. "You know, come to think of it, I've always wondered why Martin took up with FitzHerbert. He wasn't one of those as far as I know. He loved his turn with the girls hereabout. He was a strutter, you know. Always preening for the girls to get a piece of arse. I wonder if Peg didn't put him up to it somehow."

"Grope Lane doesn't seem like a place FitzHerbert would have visited."

"Nah, a swell like him wouldn't be caught dead here, although we get our share of nobs looking for some cheap and nasty fun. There are places down by the water that cater to FitzHerbert's kind."

"How would someone like FitzHerbert manage it? Finding his boys, I mean."

"There's a bath house down by the Wye Bridge in the lower town where the upper crust like to gather. A lot of hanky panky goes on in those taverns, all very quiet, you know."

"You wouldn't happen to know the name of the place FitzHerbert frequented, would you?"

"The Peacock." Nick chuckled. "Good name for it, don't you think?"

Getting to the Wye Bridge meant crossing the town and running the risk that he'd be recognized. Stephen had begun to get over his fright that he would be identified, but then he thought of a way to get where he needed to go without cutting through the town and running a risk that might be unnecessary.

He walked down Grope Lane toward the wall. The street ran along the base of the wall for a short distance and dead-ended at Hungreye Street at Saint Owen's Gate. Stephen passed through the gate, dodging a herd of goats tethered together with rope that the gate wards were counting so they could assess the appropriate toll. They were too busy with this to notice him.

Beyond the gate, Saint Owen's Church occupied the middle of the street, and sat at a fork where Saint Owen Street ran westward, the King's Greenway headed southeast, and a path skirted the edge of a water-filled moat beneath the castle's east wall. Stephen took the path.

He passed an apple and cherry orchard on the left that belonged to the King, and soon came upon the river. A mill's wheel creaked slowly with the current of the stream running through the moat.

A miller's helper was visible within the mill pouring a sack of grain into a leather funnel at the top of the grind stones. Stephen and the helper exchanged waves, then Stephen turned down the path along the top of the riverbank away from the city.

About a hundred yards down river from the mill, there was a ford, one of two that had given the city its name. This one was seldom used these days, although it was plainly visible from the high bank: ripples in the surface as the Wye flowed over the rocky bed.

Stephen waded into the river, soaking only his stockings up to the knees.

He was soon on the other bank, where the ford delivered him to a rocky beach on the south side of the river.

He walked along the edge of the river to the lower town's embankment and wooden palisade. Then he clambered up the steep riverbank, fifteen feet high if it was an inch. Entering the lower town was as simple as this.

There were no wardens upon the wall, though Stephen watched to make sure. But there was danger enough, because the eastern part of the lower town was given over to pasture and orchards belonging to the bishop. It was a severe crime to trespass upon them. Even though the bishop had been imprisoned by Montfort's supporters, there had to be someone looking after his honor's rights. However, a path ran north along the bank. People were given leave to use this path for fishing and for the hauling of barges along the river. As long as you stayed on the path you should be safe. But stray a step and you would be arrested and fined by reeves on the lookout for that very thing.

It was a good five-hundred yards from the castle ford to the Wye Bridge, a pleasant walk with the river and city to the right presenting an attractive panorama, particularly when the bishop's lush gardens and the cathedral behind them came into view, and on the left broad orchards and pasture where sheep grazed. He spotted a boy keeping watch over the herd from the top of a hayrick.

He reached the bishop's ford, which crossed the river at the cathedral and was unused by anyone now there was a fine wooden bridge just upstream. It served these days as an obstacle to heavily laden boats and barges carrying commerce up the Wye from the River Severn. Indeed, a crew was up to their knees in the river manhandling a boat over the sandbar at the ford as Stephen passed the town wharf, where more than two dozen boats were tied up at the bottom of the shear bank.

The public warehouse for storing goods was here, and north and east of Saint Martin's Church were the taverns and inns that catered to the boatmen. No sense in looking here.

The more high-toned establishments lined Saint Martin's Street. Stephen walked up and down that short street, and saw no sign indicating a tavern called the Peacock.

Bathhouses, however, usually sat near water since it was so hard to carry, and at the Wye Bridge a narrow alley lane led away to the west along the bank. Stephen found the Peacock there, last in the lane, hard against the river, tucked away out of view. It, like its customers, were the objects of official condemnation, but in practice, people looked the other way and pretended not to know as long such persons exercised discretion, and the tavern paid the sum due the alderman every month.

It was a large house and well-kept on the outside, the timbers painted a fresh, dignified black and the plaster between them a shining white with no sign of rot or mold; no fancy colors so as not to draw anyone's attention. Obviously, money was spent here, but that did not seem unusual. Hereford was a large town, and people would come here from far and wide for the chance to find safety behind the Peacock's doors to drop their masks among people who would not eye them with suspicion and contempt.

Stephen lifted the latch and entered. The tavern's hall was like that of any other tavern or bathhouse: a chamber with six tables and benches with a fireplace at the back. Doors opened on either side of the fireplace and a stair climbed to the upper floors over one of the doors.

Three fellows were drinking at one of the tables. They seemed like ordinary fellows, no different from what you'd find in any tavern, well-to-do burghers or minor gentry. They all looked at Stephen, and then away, resuming a low conversation.

A serving girl who had been hovering over the table crossed the room to Stephen. "What do you want?"

The tone suggested that he was not welcome here; his clothes were shabby compared to those by the fireplace.

"I'd like to speak to the steward," Stephen said.

"We don't need no one here," the girl said. "We're full up."

"I'm not looking for work," Stephen said. "I just have a few questions."

"Questions about what? We don't allow no questions. Be gone."

A fellow with a round pot belly secured by a dirty apron came out one of the doors by the fireplace. "What's going on, Mazzie? Trouble?"

"This lout has *questions*," the serving girl said.

"Off with you," pot belly said. "Or I'll break your head." He removed a truncheon from the small of his back and smacked it in a palm.

"Are you the steward?" Stephen asked.

"I am, if it's any business of yours. Now get out." Pot Belly took a menacing step forward.

Stephen retreated a step to give himself room to defend if needed. "I have been asked by Sir Geoffrey Curthose to help in his inquiry into Lord Rogier's death."

"He depends on *you*?" Potbelly said with disbelief. "A clod kicker?"

"I am only one of several Sir Geoffrey has sent about for that purpose."

"Why are you doing this? Curthose don't work for the honor no more. The widow discharged him first thing. The word is he was stealing goods and money from his lordship's manors."

"He still has an interest. He was his lordship's friend. He doesn't believe his lordship committed murder and killed himself. He is determined that his lordship should have a Christian burial on hallowed ground."

Potbelly frowned. "Well, he deserves that."

"You knew Sir Rogier?"

Potbelly hesitated. "He was our landlord. He owns this lane and the west side of Saint Martin's Street. A right decent man. Always ready with a kind word and a care. Not the sort of man I'd ever expect to commit murder and then suicide. He was always cheery like, you know?"

"You've had speech with him, then."

Potbelly cocked an eyebrow. "Once or twice," he said noncommittally.

"When was he in here last?"

"Oh, he never came here. He always patronized the Cauldron next door."

"The Cauldron?" Stephen asked, puzzled. Then he remembered the sign over the door of the neighboring house, a red cauldron tipping on the side with blue water pouring out.

"Our competition, so to speak."

"Another bathhouse?"

"My, you are quick. No wonder Sir Geoffrey employs you."

"I see. And the Cauldron, does it …?"

"It caters to the ordinary sort. Not our clientele. We're special. You're not from around here, are you."

"No."

"Where you from, then?"

"Nowhere. Up north."

"Where up north?"

"Chester."

"You don't sound like Chester born. You sound right Herefordshire or I'm a flea."

"Raised in Shrewsbury."

"Huh. And you're here for Curthose?"

"That's right."

Potbelly considered these things silently for a few moments, his rather piggish face screwed up at the effort that this cost. "Come out back with me."

Potbelly led Stephen through the left doorway by the fireplace down a long corridor. Chambers with tubs in them lined both sides of the corridor, visible when the curtains across the doorways were not drawn.

They came out the back door to a path on the top of the embankment that sloped precipitously to the green river.

"I did not get your name," Stephen said.

"Quentin. You're not a clod-kicker. Who are you?"

"Let's leave that for now. This is intended to be a discrete inquiry. What do you have to add?"

"Curthose thinks that his lordship didn't kill himself?"

"There is good reason to think that he didn't."

"What do you need to know?"

"Sir Rogier was seen leaving through Wydemarsh Gate during the evening that he died, four days ago now. He was with the boy Martin, and one other. My informant did not get a look at the third fellow's face. I need to know who he was."

"More likely a she."

"A *she?*" This took Stephen aback. It was not what he had expected.

Quentin sighed. "Let me tell you how it worked. His lordship has a private chamber in the Cauldron. Martin comes over and selects one of our guests to tarry with Sir Rogier. They come out the door," he gestured to the door they had just exited, "and cross over to the Cauldron." Quentin pointed to the path that ran along the lip of the bank. "His lordship's chamber is in the back on the left. It's easy to go in and out without attracting notice, and since his lordship owns a share in both the Cauldron and the Peacock we didn't ask no questions."

"You said this person was a woman."

"Yeah. Never seen her before a week ago. She showed up with a troupe of players. They entertained at the castle and then at the market. For some reason, she and two of the boys from the troupe hung out here for a few days."

"But I thought Sir Rogier was inclined to men."

"He was. He liked to give Martin presents. Martin said he enjoyed watching. He was right sweet on Martin. I warned him that any spawn of Squinty Peg's couldn't be trusted, but he was smitten. Deeply smitten. In love, perhaps. Martin was a charmer."

"And Martin went both ways."

"Well, I think he went more one way than the other, and the other was for the money. That rat would do anything for money, like the rest of the brood."

"It seems you didn't like him."

"I don't like any of Squinty Peg's brood. Greedy to the bone and utterly without conscience, the lot of them. And there are lot of them."

"What was this woman's name?"

"Mary. At least, that's the name she gave out."

"What does she look like?"

"She's a tiny thing. Red hair, freckles. Quite pretty. Limber as an eel. She went up to the roof and walked a handstand along the peak on a bet."

"And after she went off with FitzHerbert and Martin, you never saw her again?"

"Not a sign."

Chapter 9

Quentin returned to the Peacock.

Stephen stared for many moments at the translucent green water of the Wye flowing lazily beneath his feet, long water plants stirring in the current like banners. He tried to make sense of what Quentin had told him, to fit it into a pattern that explained the deaths of FitzHerbert and Martin. But try as he could, he was unable to see how a slender girl could have killed them.

Unless those two boys helped somehow. They could have followed this Mary as she walked with FitzHerbert and Martin to the lord's house, and she could somehow have seen they got into it. Or they could have killed the two along the road and carried them into the house. Or killed them on the doorstep. They would have had to kill FitzHerbert to get the key around his neck. Or would they? He felt like he was running in circles.

He had four hours of daylight left, time enough to do a lot of work, if he only knew what to do.

Then Stephen remembered something Quentin said: she had belonged to a troupe of players. These were jugglers, acrobats, mimes, puppet masters, and actors who traveled from one town to another staging performances that often took place on the bed of a wagon and the ground around it. They made their money by donations given to a member circulating through the crowd. But some also employed urchins and the unsavory to cut purses as well.

If he could find out where they went, he might catch up with this Mary and her boys.

As Stephen walked up the path along the river to the timber-and-stone gate towers on this side of the Wye Bridge, he thought about how to make this search. He had a feeling that the town bailiffs would know where the troupe had stayed, but he couldn't ask one of them. It would require making inquiries at every inn in the city. He doubted that the players would have taken shelter at one of the inns without the gates. While the cost of lodging was less, it would have been more than made up by the tolls charged at the gates for the entry into town.

Stephen walked down Saint Martin's Street and called at the two inns there, and learned nothing. That left those in the city proper. It meant he would have to walk about in daylight, where he could be recognized. The possibility of having to return to the gaol pit filled him with dread. But he had no choice, did he?

So he crossed the Wye Bridge, where small boys were walking on the railings to avoid wagons laden with bundles and casks from the wharf, and went up Bridge Street to its three inns to continue the search.

At the West Gate, Stephen discovered that a path ran along the base of the wall at the back edges of the rear gardens. This allowed him to reach each gate and walk up the main streets leading from them. He was able to work his way around the town to all the inns, which were by the gates for the good custom. The only one he wouldn't be able to reach using this method was the inn at Cabosches Street and Canon Lane. But it was unlikely the troupe stayed there. That inn catered to clerks having business at Hereford cathedral or pilgrims.

Many innkeepers knew of the visiting troupe, having seen the players perform in the market. But none knew where they had lodged.

It was nearly sundown when Stephen reached Saint Owen's Gate on the east side of town, where he had started that morning. There were two inns here, the Hare, at the corner of Grope Lane and Hungreye Street, and the Green Turtle.

Stephen stopped at the window of the Hare. A matron turned away from the bar to face him. "What can I get for you?" she asked, smoothing her apron. She was a stout woman with a friendly face who reminded Stephen of Gilbert's wife, Edith.

"I'll have an ale," he said.

The matron upended a small cask over a wooden cup. "Here you go."

Stephen gulped the contents, set the cup down, and motioned for the matron to fill it again.

"You look tired," the matron said, as she refilled the cup. "Come far?"

"I've been walking all day," Stephen said, mindful of how his bad foot was aching. He downed that cup too, and wiped a spill off his chin.

"What brings you to Hereford?" The matron frowned. "You look familiar. You been here before?"

"Once or twice." In fact, Stephen had passed within sight of the Hare when he went out Saint Owen's Gate that morning. "I'm looking for a troupe of players. They would have passed through here a few days ago."

"Oh, I remember them. A rowdy bunch they were, drinking and fussing into the night after they had to leave Grope Lane, 'cos of the curfew. The bailiffs had to come by several times on account of them."

"They stayed here?"

"Nah. Up at the Turtle. I could hear them from my room all that way, so you can imagine the racket."

"Do you know where they went?"

"They didn't bother to tell me. We weren't on good terms. I was one who summoned the bailiffs. A couple of those boys and that girl found out and came down here to complain." She rapped on the window shutter, which was open downward to form a shelf or table a little over waist high. "She jumped onto me shutter, if you can believe that, and almost broke it off." The matron shook her head. "I went to shove her away and she leaped off with a back flip. If I hadn't been so pissed at them, I'd have marveled at it."

"She is something, isn't she?"

"You know her?"

"Not yet. But I will."

"Why're you interested in that lot? They steal something of yours?"

"Something like that. Thanks for the ale and conversation. You've been very helpful."

The sign for the Green Turtle, a green turtle upending a cup and spilling most of it, jutted into Hungreye Street about fifty yards away where it could catch the eye of any traveler coming through the gate. It was at the corner of Castle Street.

Stephen was halfway there before he stopped. The bailiffs had marched Stephen right by it on the way to gaol. He remembered the stares he got from the patrons inside, and anyone still there, like the staff, was likely to remember him.

He dared not go any farther. He would have to get someone else to inquire about the troupe at the Green Turtle. He retreated into Grope Lane, feeling whipped, despising himself for his cowardice, and passed down its length toward Old Street.

The taverns and whorehouses were bursting in customers, the business spilling into the street, the lane filled with shouting, singing and general clamor. A dice game was going on beneath the windows of an alehouse. One player did not like the result of the throw, shoved the thrower off the blanket, and tried to seize the winnings. Daggers flashed and one of the players clouted the fellow on the head with a pommel and down he went, unconscious. The players rolled him off the blanket and resumed the game. Stephen glimpsed a whore on her knees in an alley servicing a fellow with his shirt pulled up, and watched one boy distract a man who was already drunk while another cut his purse with the deftness of a surgeon. A lad loomed before Stephen holding out a bowl, crying that he was starving and begging for aid — "Please, sir! A farthing just to tide us over till me mum gets well!" Stephen skipped around him before his partner could get a hand on his belt pouch. He spotted another lad with his wand out as if he were preparing to pee. The lad looked at Stephen with an appraising eye. Stephen gave him a wide berth. The boy swung around and peed on the feet of a merchant coming behind Stephen. The merchant cried out in anger at this violation, shaking his finger at the peeing lad and threatening the crack of doom upon him. The child pretended to cower in fear, while another lad cut the merchant's purse from behind. Stephen probably should have done something to stop this crime, but that would have drawn attention to himself. Besides, it was rather interesting to watch such artists at work, as long as he did not become a target.

A pair of bailiffs strolled toward Stephen. He pulled down his hat, but neither bailiff paid him any attention, as they were intent on a whore bending out a window, naked breasts to the evening breeze, beckoning at a young wealthy fellow wearing an embroidered maroon cloak in the lane to sample Sodom's offerings.

"You there!" one of the bailiffs shouted. "Cover up!"

"But not too quickly," the other muttered, giving his friend a nudge.

"My duty is done," the friend said, and they moved on as the wealthy young fellow stepped to the window to sample what was on display like a buyer of apples fingering the apples. The girl then withdrew. The young fellow lingered in the street for a moment, then entered the house.

Up the street, a large crowd was gathered about a platform with posts at its four corners, each of them with an oil lamp in a bowl at the top to provide illumination. Stephen was surprised to see Peg on a large, throne-like chair on the platform. Her dress was different this evening but as fine as before. She was hearing grievances from people in the crowd. At first, Stephen thought it was serious, but when he got close enough to hear what people were saying, he realized it was a farce. A fellow accused of having relations with a sheep was sentenced to drop his hose and prance about showing his naked arse while baaing like the violated sheep. Instead of doing so sullenly, as one might expect, the accused laughed, showed his bum, performed a drunken dance, and had his cup refilled. Peg tossed him a half-penny for the display. A woman then accused another man of masturbating in public. This was a popular charge and drew a thunderous laugh from the crowd. The accusation was put to a vote and this accused was convicted. Stephen drew out of earshot before he heard the sentence.

Stephen reached Olde Street and turned into it. Grope Lane's tumult gradually subsided as he drew away.

He crossed the open space where Old Street, Bye Street and Jews Lane came together, and entered the dark maw of Jews Lane. The lane ran along the base of the city wall for a short distance and then curved left. Stephen came around the curve and at last reached Theo and Sarah's house.

He knocked on the door. It was some time in opening. Theo stood on the threshold.

"God's blood," he snarled. "You've a nerve coming here! The whole city knows you're on the loose!"

But instead of closing the door in Stephen's face, Theo grasped him by the shirt as Sarah had done, and yanked him inside.

Chapter 10

"You should have flown first chance you had," Theo fumed.

Stephen, Gilbert, Sarah and Theo were all gathered at the Tennets' dinner table in the faint light of a fading hearth fire, the children having been sent upstairs to bed. The Tennets did not bother with candles or oil lamps to save on the expense, even though recently they had come into money. Unlike some, they were careful about where their pennies went.

Theo went on. "Someone checked the pit this afternoon. Now the whole city is on the lookout for you. What are you up to, anyway?"

"I've a job to do."

"A job worth your life? A job worth my life and the lives of my family?"

"I'll be gone this very night," Stephen said. "I won't trouble you any longer. But there are things yet to be done."

"That's a relief, though a small one." Theo glanced sourly at Sarah. "You should never have let him in."

"I had to," she said. "After what he's done for Harry."

"Harry," Theo muttered. "That no good layabout."

"He's not a layabout any longer, thanks to Sir Stephen," Sarah shot back.

"What things?" Gilbert asked.

"We've a letter to find," Stephen said.

"What kind of letter?"

Stephen explained about Montfort's missing letter.

"Ah, that explains Lady Margaret's interest. And why Walter instructed me to come here. You need help."

"I do," Stephen said. "More so now I've been found out."

"How can I help?" Gilbert asked.

"A troupe of players stayed at the Green Turtle by Saint Owen's Gate. We need to find out where they went."

"A troupe of players?" Gilbert asked, surprised. "That's very odd."

"Players are always odd. Why more so now?"

"Because some of those players were found murdered just outside the city."

And Gilbert went on to tell the story.

Michael was seven, almost old enough to work full time. He had been employed as a clod-breaker during the spring plowing, but so far he had avoided the hard work suffered by his older brothers and sisters, although he was often stuck with chores about the house like carrying water, weeding the garden, and scaring away crows. But he was already an enterprising shirker of work and knew to get out of sight early in the morning before his mother could think of something profitable to occupy his time.

He had a favorite spot where he liked to hide. It was in a small grove about two-hundred yards east of the FitzHerbert house on Frere Lane. There was a large oak here with a crook between two great limbs big enough for him to sit down in it. If anyone came by, he could not be seen from that high up.

Timmins the collie went with him. Michael was not happy about being followed at first, but then gave up trying to drive Timmins away. And after a while, he grew glad for the company.

A short distance into the little wood, he smelled an awful smell: something dead. It was a pretty strong smell, and he wasn't sure that he would be able to stand it long, which meant there would be no hiding in the tree.

He turned away, considering where to go instead, when Timmins bounded deeper into the wood and began baying loudly.

Michael went to collect Timmins and found her lunging toward and recoiling from a piece of disturbed earth, continuing to yelp nonstop. The stench of death was strong enough to make him gag.

"Cut that out," Michael said to the dog. "Leave it."

But the dog did not heed his commands.

The dog began digging in the disturbed earth.

"Enough!" Michael snapped and grasped the dog by the scruff of her neck to pull her away.

But then Michael noticed a white object in the hole that dog had dug. He bent closer to see what it was, despite the smell.

It was a hand, or part of one, the fingers swollen and waxy.

Michael reached out to smooth dirt away from the hand but then thought better of it.

He ran back to Frere Lane and pelted toward Wydemarsh Street and home.

Michael told his mother about the body. At first, she looked at him squinty eyed, as if she didn't believe him.

"Show me," she said.

Off they went to Frere Lane, with Timmins and the last of her puppies as an escort.

"In there," Michael said when they reached the copse.

His mother wrinkled her nose at the smell. If she doubted him before, the odor gave evidence that he was not telling tales.

She advanced into the grove.

She took one look at the hand in the hole, grasped Michael by the collar, and dragged him back to the lane.

Michael's mother went straight to Wydemarsh Gate and told the wardens there what Michael had found.

One of the wardens ran off to the castle to fetch the coroner while another went to the hundred alderman to summon the local jury.

It took an hour for the jurymen of the hundred to show up, with still no sign of the coroner. Rather than wait any longer, since they were all working men and the delay cost them money, the jurors proceeded to the death site, followed by a considerable crowd that had gathered outside the gate at the news.

Gilbert heard the commotion in the street as he fretted away his time with a tankard of ale, waiting for Walter to show up and tell him what to do. He watched out the window of his inn as the crowd collected at the gate. People were talking excitedly about something. He heard the words body, coroner, and jurors mentioned through the hubbub. He downed the last of his ale, which was quite good and sweet and very fresh. Then he went out to see what the fuss was about.

It did not take long for Gilbert to piece together from random comments what the jurors faced.

The mass flowed around the corner of the lane, which at the Wydemarsh end was called Hospital Lane, and continued past the FitzHerbert manor house, where the lane's named changed.

Gilbert paused at the manor house because an odd sight caught his eye. There was a large, blue-painted wagon in the yard and four rough-looking men were struggling to unload a fellow on a stretcher from the back. The man was big and massively muscled. He had auburn almost red hair, with a jutting chin. He wore a tailored green coat, but the rest of him was concealed by a linen sheet, except for a red-stocking foot that had a splint at the ankle. Lady Isabel and Lady Madeline fussed over him as the servants lifted the stretcher from the bed of the wagon, and carried him into the house.

A striking, richly dressed woman, in a maroon gown a riot of golden embroidery with blue silk sleeves on her under gown watched the cortege approach from the doorway to the house. She had to be in her late thirties, and so beautiful that Gilbert halted in the road to take in the vision: pointed chin emphasized by the veil about her head and neck, graceful hands clasp but then one rising in a wave.

Then she noticed Gilbert staring and flinty hardness replaced the pleasure as she backed into the house.

Gilbert wondered what to make of it as he hurried to catch up with the crowd, which had almost reached the grove.

The crowd went in after Michael, his mother, and the jury, nearly packing it to the full. Gilbert had to worm his way through the press to the edge of it, where a ring had formed about a hastily dug grave, no mean feat for a portly man who had trouble conducting worming of any kind.

One of the jurors had brought a hoe and a shovel, and two jurors got to work uncovering the body. It was not buried very deeply; only a few inches of soil had been thrown upon it. When it had been uncovered, two jurors put on gloves and pulled the body from the grave. The smell was so foul that many people held the hems of their shirts or gowns over their noses.

But the big surprise was that beneath this body was another.

The jurymen laid the bodies side-by-side and brushed the dirt from the faces.

"Anyone know them?" the chief juryman asked.

"I seen 'em," said a man a couple of rows in. He was tall and could see over the heads of those in front of him. "They're some of those players, the ones at the market these past few days."

Many in the crowd called their agreement, recognizing them now, even though their features were distorted with the decay of death.

"And they were men?" Stephen asked when Gilbert got to this point in his story.

"That's right," Gilbert said. "Why?"

"No woman?" Stephen asked.

"No," Gilbert said. "I can tell a woman from a man, even one that's been dead several days and once buried."

"How were they killed?"

"Stabbed in the back and their throats cut for good measure."

"They were surprised by whoever killed them, then."

"It would seem so. Why are you so concerned about a woman?"

"Because there had to be a woman involved." Stephen told those at the table about what he had learned at the Peacock.

"She couldn't have killed two men," Sarah said.

"One, maybe, but not two," Gilbert agreed. "She had to have had help. I wonder why they were murdered in the first place — ah! A falling out over the stolen money."

"That seems the best idea," Stephen said. "Or to silence them for their part in the murders of Martin and Sir Rogier."

"But why not kill the girl as well?"

"Perhaps she got away."

"Or she was in league with the killers," Gilbert said.

Stephen sighed. "There are too many possibilities to count. But if we can find her, perhaps we can shed light on the truth."

"How are we going to do that?" Gilbert asked.

"The troupe took lodgings at the Green Turtle," Stephen said. "It's an inn on Hungreye Street up from Saint Owen's Gate."

At Gilbert's puzzled expression, Theo said, "Everyone in Hereford knows where it is."

"Someone needs to go there first thing tomorrow morning," Stephen said, "and see if they left any clue where they were going next."

"I suppose you expect me to do it," Gilbert said.

"I can't very well do it. I'll be recognized."

"And what about you?"

"I need to think of a way to get out of the city."

Chapter 11

The simplest way to get out of a city at night undetected was to go over the wall. But the wall was twenty feet high. Stephen risked turning an ankle if not breaking a leg from that sort of drop. He might use a rope, but that would leave evidence that someone had taken the route, and suspicion would immediately fall upon him.

He thought about using the bishop's ford, which crossed the Wye near the Wye Bridge. He could pass through the bishop's pasture and get over the palisade enclosing the lower town.

But then he thought of a way out that did not involve getting wet. The problem here was the same as using the wall, a ten-foot drop — not that far a fall, but again not something Stephen wanted to attempt in the dark.

"Theo," Stephen asked, "do you have a rope?"

"Why?"

"I'd like to borrow it."

"I suppose, if it will help get rid of you."

Theo produced a coil of rope from a chest in the corner.

Stephen looped the rope around a stair and secured it with a horse knot, which involved tying a knot in which one end could bear any amount of force, but a tug on the other end released the knot. He tried the knot to see if it would hold his weight. It did. He tugged the free end and the knot unraveled.

"I'll leave it behind the Trumpet, where Gilbert boarded the horses," Stephen said.

"Thanks. Ropes cost a lot of money," Theo said.

Gilbert contemplated the rope as Stephen coiled it. "It occurs to me that our killer could have escaped FitzHerbert's house that way."

"It occurred to me, too," Stephen said. "Remember how the bed had been moved slightly? The rope was tied to the bed and the weight of the killer pulled it off. Everyone knows how to make this knot, well almost everyone apart from you. I don't know why I didn't think of it before."

Jews Street was silent when Stephen stepped into the night. No lights twinkled through cracks in the shutters, and no muffled voices could be heard. There was no moon yet, and when it rose in the wee hours it would be nothing but a waning sliver even if the gathering clouds did not obscure it. It was, Stephen realized, the first day of September, and there was already a nip in the air.

He slipped along Jews Street keeping close to the houses, alert for the slightest sound or glimmer of light, especially any glimmer. The night watch patrolled the city in pairs and carried a lantern suspended from a pole to light the way.

He paused at Wydemarsh Street, looking one way and then the other. Seeing and hearing nothing, he crept out into Wydemarsh and went south until he reached the first right. He turned there into Frenschemanne Street and crept as far as All Saints Church, where he went left across High Street to the little alley of Norgate.

Stephen had barely entered the alley when something struck his good foot, tripping him. He fell on his face. Someone leaped upon his back, and snaked a forearm around his neck, cutting off his wind. The head of his assailant was close to Stephen's left ear, hot breath upon it. He reached up, grasped the man's hair, turned to free his right arm, and drove his fingers into the man's eyes. The attacker shrieked and let go.

It felt as though Stephen merely pushed off the ground and bounded to his feet, and he was surrounded by others barely discernable in the dark.

They had not been ready for his escape from the hold on the ground and for an instant did not respond. Then one of them raised a scarcely visible hand wielding a scarcely visible club. Stephen kicked the club man in the groin with his bad foot, pivoted and parried a punch and responded with one of his own, pivoted the other way while drawing his dagger, and stabbed the last man with a low thrust to the stomach and finished him a high thrust to the neck. Meanwhile, the man he'd kicked in the groin was struggling to his feet. Stephen drove the dagger under the man's chin into his brain. The clubman collapsed without a sound. Stephen would have killed the man he had punched as well, but that fellow had run off down the alley. That left the man Stephen had poked in the eyes, who had not stopped screaming all this short time. Stephen stabbed him too to shut him up, collected the rope from the ground, and ran as well as he could with his bad foot, a sort of limping trot, toward Brode Street which opened up at the south end of the alley.

At the mouth of the alley, Stephen slowed to a walk. The screaming will have got the attention of the watch, not to mention all the householders hereabout and it would only be moments before someone came out to investigate the disturbance. Anyone seen running would immediately be thought to be complicit, and detained, especially if the hue and cry was raised.

Stephen turned right onto Behynderthewall Street. The original plan had been to take the first left, Wrotehale Street, to Bridge Street, but he passed it and instead turned left down an alley called Plow Lane. He heard voices calling "Out! Out!" in the direction of Norgate and a bell began clanging — the watch sounding the alarm — but he thought he might be far enough away by now that if anyone looked out they would not connect him with the fresh killings. It had been bad luck to run into a bunch of robbers when he had hoped to reach the Wye Bridge undetected.

Plow Lane emptied into Westgate Street, with the gate not far away to the right and Saint Nicholas' Church an island in the street to the left.

Stephen was tempted to take the direct route, for the mouth of Bridge Street opened beyond the church. But he hesitated.

A good thing, too, because five gate wardens, alerted by the alarm bell, trotted by him and went around the church.

It occurred to Stephen that this left only one man at the gate, since the royal decree of 1252 required a complement of six be maintained at a city's gates. It was the normal duty of the wardens to keep watch outward rather than inward, so Stephen might not be seen.

On this uncertain premise, Stephen tip-toed down West Gate Street and turned into the gap between the first and second houses up from the gate. He crossed a back garden and vaulted the wicker fence to the path along the base of the wall. He knelt, listening for anyone to shout at his trespass, but no one did.

Confident that he had not been seen after all, Stephen padded along the path to the point where the wall turned sharply east, and in a few moments he was kneeling in the dark where the city wall ended at Bridge Street by the foot of the bridge, surprised that he was so out of breath.

Stephen gulped air and stepped onto the bridge.

The drop from the bridge to the lower bank of the river was about fifteen feet or so, give or take. Stephen draped the rope around a support beam and made his horse knot. He dropped both ends. Then he slipped over the railing and lowered himself to the sand. A tug on one end, the knot unraveled, and he coiled the rope.

"What you up to?" a man's gravel voice inquired from the darkness beneath the bridge.

"Trying to make a quiet getaway, what does it look like? But that seems to be impossible," Stephen said, startled. Vagrants sometimes slept beneath the bridges at Ludlow, but he had not expected to find anyone beneath Wye Bridge because it was hard to reach from outside the city. "If you don't say you saw me, I'll not mention this conversation."

"Fair enough. Just don't like my sleep disturbed, is all."

"My apologies."

"Accepted."

Stephen climbed the steep bank to the base of the city wall and followed it to the town ditch, which ran northward with the wall itself. The ditch was a deep V-shape with water at the bottom; not good walking. He crossed the ditch and struck out into the fields of the Grey Friars' Priory.

Presently, he stumbled onto a road whose name he could not remember. The West Gate loomed to the right, visible against the sky. Stephen waved at the invisible warden in the towers, and continued walking up a cart track to the north.

The track ended at Above Eigne Road, where a stream coursed beside the street, emptying into the castle ditch eventually to meet the Wye on the other side of the city.

Beyond were fields, a mist beginning to collect upon them.

Stephen trudged around to the north side of Hereford to a great field that stretched off into the night without any visible boundaries, and found a hayrick near the road to Leominster that had not yet been taken in. It was made of new-mowed grass and smelled fresh and good. He burrowed into the rick, feeling safe like a fox in his hole even if that was an illusion, and settled down for the remainder of the night.

He was so tired that he was asleep in moments.

Chapter 12

The clank of a bell woke Stephen. He stuck his head out of his burrow to establish that the carrier of the bell was a sheep, and saw that sunrise was near. It was a good thing that sheep had come along, otherwise he might have slept for several hours more, and then he might have been seen crossing the field in daylight.

The place appointed for the meeting with Gilbert was a stand of trees just up the road from Hospital Lane, where FitzHerbert's house was visible in the distance.

Stephen settled to the ground to wait, his back to a tree.

A foot prodded him awake.

"Time to get up," Gilbert said. "We need to be away. The entire city is aflame with news of you. Dozens of people must have passed you just this morning. It's a miracle no one's noticed you here, just waiting to be snapped up without the slightest struggle."

Stephen climbed to his feet. "Did you learn anything?"

"I did, in fact. Our players are talkative people."

"Well?"

"Patience, my good friend. I know it's hard for you, but try it for once. First you must tell me if you had anything to do with that disturbance in Norgate Lane last night. The whole city is in an uproar over it, and you are the chief suspect. I must say, it's done wonders for your reputation as a ruffian and man to be reckoned with."

"At this point, I'm not confessing to anything. FitzAllan is sure to add that to my list of crimes anyway. The truth doesn't seem to count for much anymore."

"Have it your way. I thought you'd enjoy the boost in reputation. I heard some harpist at the Trumpet making a song about your escape and the slaughter, and it isn't even the third hour yet." Gilbert wrinkled his nose. "Now that I think about it, the song was more an excuse to make fun of FitzAllan than laud you. Well, then, our players are headed to our old stomping grounds."

"Ludlow?"

"I know of no other old stomping grounds."

"You're sure?"

"That's what the stable boy overheard them to say."

"What, exactly, did he hear?"

"One of the players asked a merchant as they left which road to take to Ludlow and how far was it."

"And you believe it to be true?"

"Why not?"

"Perhaps they meant to be overheard to throw any pursuit off the scent."

"And you accuse me of overthinking things!"

"Still, I suppose it's all we have."

Stephen mounted his horse while Gilbert struggled to climb onto his mule, which shied away so that he stumbled and only a desperate grasp of the saddle pommel prevented a fall.

"You're not getting any better at that," Stephen said.

"It's not for lack of practice these days with all the scurrying about I'm forced to do at some unkind person's behest — to London and back, trips down the great river! —"

"And into the great river," Stephen muttered.

"— but she sees me coming and wants to torment me. Why does everyone use me so roughly?"

"Because it's so easy?"

"Oh, do be quiet. You are interfering with my concentration."

But at last, Gilbert was aboard.

"Hold on tight," Stephen said. "It's time to go home."

It was twenty miles to Ludlow, a journey that normally took a day, but Stephen and Gilbert covered the distance in four hours of hard riding without Gilbert falling, although he came close twice.

Stephen's horse could have kept up the pace for another ten miles or more, but the mule had had enough and stopped dead on the slope above the River Temes bridge.

Gilbert stepped down and tried to lead the mule on foot, but she dug in and would not budge until Stephen tapped her on the flank with his whip. Instead of walking forward, as Gilbert intended, the mule bolted away, knocking Gilbert on his arse, raced across the bridge, and dashed on up Lower Broad Street, stirrups flapping, only stopping at the gate, where Gip, the toothless warden, caught her.

Gilbert observed the flight with eyes narrowed in uncharacteristic fury. "I wonder if mules make good eating."

"Nah, too tough."

"Not if you boil it long enough, I'll wager."

Stephen crossed the bridge with Gilbert limping a bit behind.

"Good Lord!" cried Gip, when Stephen bent to retrieve the mule's reins. "Look who it is! We heard you was in prison! Murder, they say!"

"Good day to you, too," Stephen said, depositing a farthing on Gip's outstretched palm. "I am such an amiable fellow. Why do people seem to think me capable of murder? Anyway, thanks for catching Nellie. I was in prison, but I have been released."

"You don't say." Gip did not sound convinced.

"The Sheriff has a high sense of justice and a respect for the law."

"That's not what I hear."

"You won't tell anyone that you've seen me, will you, Gip?"

Gip's face screwed up. "I'd like to, sir. But I have my duty. I'll have to."

"Give me an hour or so before you send word to Henle at the castle. Can you do that?"

"An hour, sir. I'll give you that."

"Ah, and here's a penny for your trouble."

"Thank you, sir!"

Stephen stood in front of his house in Bell Lane, which was only a door down the slope toward Broad Street and across from the Broken Shield Inn. He had not been in the house long, but it had begun to feel like home. It was good to be back.

He gave the mare's reins to Gilbert, who led the horse and his trusty mule into the inn's yard.

He smelled fire coming from the front of the house, which was Harry's shop. This was alarming, since there should be no fires in the front. The shutters were down even though it was a Sunday, so Stephen looked in. Harry and Joan, the pretty young housekeeper, were crouched over a board resting on the dirt floor on which an ember was burning at the end. Her hand rested on Harry's shoulder in a familiar way that Stephen had not noticed between them before. It took a moment to register that Harry was burning in the bowl of what would become a wooden spoon.

"You're going to get in trouble working on Sunday," Stephen said.

Both Harry and Joan jumped at the sound of his voice. "Good Lord! You're back!" Harry exclaimed. "You're supposed to be in gaol!"

"I decided that I didn't like it, so I broke out."

"Just another thing to add to your growing list of crimes." Harry looked bitter. "It looks like we're going to have to go back to the stable, if Edith Wistwode will even allow such a thing." When Harry was a beggar, he had lived on the Wistwodes' sufferance in their stable behind the inn. "You won't be here longer than necessary to pack your things. The new tenant won't be as malleable as you, or as lenient on the rent."

"You're saying I'm soft?"

"No, just easy to manipulate for someone as cunning as me."

"Well, I'm not running. Where's Ida? Is she home?" What affection there had been between Ida and her mother, Elysande, had evaporated at William's death and Stephen's succession to Hafton Manor, and she had been living with him in the Ludlow townhouse since then.

Joan and Harry looked troubled.

"She's not here," Joan said.

"Lady Elysande and some of FitzAllan's men came the day you left," Harry said. He pulled himself up to the bench at the window. "She said she just wanted to visit. So Mistress Bartelot let them in. But they seized Lady Ida straightway and rode off with her and Mistress Bartelot."

"She didn't want to go," Joan said. "But they forced her."

"Where did they go?" Stephen asked.

"We heard north," Harry said.

"To Clun is my guess," Joan said. "A friend of mine saw them riding out the Corve Street Gate."

"Except Lady Elysande didn't go that way," Harry said. "I talked to Gip and he said she went back home."

"How did he know it was back home?" Stephen asked.

"Well," Harry said, "the manor lies south, doesn't it?"

"It doesn't matter," Stephen said. "She turned up in Hereford. Accused me of killing my brother."

"We heard you'd been accused of that," Joan said. "Such nonsense."

"Deadly nonsense, I'm afraid," Stephen said.

"Nobody around here believes the charge," Joan said. "Everybody knows FitzAllan hates you."

"Except those who want to," Harry said. "But there's only a few of them. The Wattepasses' friends, mostly. And that fellow Humbert Thame. I heard he's been carrying on about you, saying that we've finally seen your true colors, stuff like that. If I was a little taller, I'd bust his lip." Thame was grocer with a shop at the Bull Ring.

"Ida wouldn't allow such an accusation to stand!" Joan said.

"That's obviously why she was taken off to Clun," Stephen said. "So she won't have the chance." It was clear that Elysande and FitzAllan had been in touch about the accusation long before his arrest. His invitation to Hereford probably had been part of the plan: to bring him to a place where he had no support so that he could be arrested and gaoled without trouble. He had hoped to find Ida here to enlist her help in refuting the charge. But Elysande and FitzAllan had thought ahead about that.

"Don't move back to the stable yet," Stephen went on. "There may be things I can do in the end to set things right. But the first thing I have to do is see Walter Henle. Do you remember where we put the shovel?"

"It's in the back shed," Joan said. "I'll fetch it."

Stephen and Harry met Joan in the corner of the hall where Harry slept. Stephen noted that there were two pallets on the floor there rather than one. He pulled them aside without comment and started digging for his money box. He lifted it out of the hole. He opened the lid and started counting pennies onto Harry's blanket.

He counted out sixty shillings, which he tied up in a cloth Joan fetched from the kitchen, since he had no pouches big enough to carry such a massive sum.

Then he returned the money box to the hole and covered it up.

"What are you doing to do with all that money?" Harry asked.

"See if Henle can be bought."

"I've always thought that was possible, but are you sure that's enough? He is the greedy sort. And your back's against the wall."

"I hope it's enough. But there's always more in the hole."

Walter Henle was the constable of Ludlow Castle. He had been a close friend of Percival FitzAllan, earl of Arundel, but when FitzAllan switched sides, they found themselves enemies, for Henle's employer who held the castle, the Geneville family, were staunchly for the King. Therein lay the opportunity, or so Stephen calculated.

Stephen walked up to the castle as fully armed as if he were going to battle. People on the High Street going about their business at the shops paused at the sight of him. There was a great deal of shocked conversation which he could not hear, and fingers pointed in amazement. But he wanted people to notice him and see that he wasn't running away.

The two gate wardens on duty at the main gate had long been on their feet when Stephen got there.

"Afternoon, sir," one of them, Randel, said. "You look splendid. What's the occasion?"

Stephen ignored the question. "Is Henle here?"

"He's at the hall. We sent a runner to the hall as soon as we saw it was you. Dinner should be over by now. I doubt he's wandered off. You know how he likes his ale after dinner."

"Good. I won't have to pry him out of the privy," Stephen said. "Good day to you, boys."

"And you, sir. Good luck at whatever you're up to."

Stephen crossed the outer bailey to the inner gate, conscious of the eyes of the watch on him as well as those from the barrack and stables along the outer wall.

Four armed men of the inner watch met him at the inner gate.

"Sorry, sir," the sergeant in charge said. "I'll have to ask you to surrender your weapons."

"Then you'll have to take them. Where is Henle?"

"In the hall. Please don't put up a fight, sir. We're ordered to arrest you."

"You can try to arrest me, if need be, after I've had words with Henle. Not before."

He didn't wait for an answer. He marched past them around the round chapel to the stairs to the hall. They hurried after him, but did not attempt either to get within arms' reach or to deprive him of his sword.

Stephen mounted the steps and entered the hall.

Henle was sitting in his high-backed chair behind the great table at the far end of the hall. Servants were clearing up the mess left from dinner: sweeping the floor, wiping down tables and taking them apart for stacking against the wall. Here and there people were clustered in conversation while waiting for Henle to finish his ale and for the post-dinner Sunday festivities to start. People turned to watch.

"Good of you to receive me, Sir Walter," Stephen said.

"Are you looking for a fight, Attebrook?" Henle asked. His stubby fingers curled around his cup. He had a great blocky head resting upon a great blocky body that must have been formidable in his youth. But now he was pushing forty and the softer life of a castle constable and manor steward had added to his bulk, but around the waist, which was out of view below the table.

"Only if you want to start one," Stephen said.

Henle eyed the sack of money in Stephen's left hand, his non-sword hand. "Then why are you here?"

Stephen laid the sack on the table. "To negotiate."

"You know that's not how the law is enforced."

"Don't take me for a child, or a peasant, Henle."

Henle's fingers fidgeted on the tabletop. "It's curious that Lady Ida abjured her honor for you after Sir William's death. Many suspect you exerted unreasonable and unfair pressure on that poor girl."

"I did nothing of the kind. She is not the issue of my brother's body. She is his step-daughter."

"That may be true as far as it goes, but Elysande is saying that William adopted Ida and made her his heir."

This was the first Stephen had heard of this. William had loved Ida like his own daughter. So, it would not have been surprising that he had made Ida his heir. But neither Elysande nor Ida had ever said anything about it. If they had, Stephen would not have asserted a claim to his home manor, Hafton.

"What proof does she have of this?"

"I understand she has a writ, signed and sealed by William."

"If she has that, why bring a murder charge, if not to invalidate my claim with a conviction? She could have more easily have brought suit instead."

"I don't know. Suits cost money. You were a lawyer once. You know that better than anyone. Perhaps the charge is true. I am sure she loved him deeply."

"Like a pig loves the butcher."

"That is cruel."

"You know it's true."

Henle shrugged. "What I know doesn't count for much."

"You're right. What you know or not doesn't count. I came to remind you what side you're on," Stephen said. "I got my commission as coroner directly from the hands of Prince Edward. In these especially troubled times, he will not be pleased to learn I have been deprived of that commission by a Montfort supporter — and accused by that same man of trumped up charges of murder."

"What's that got to do with me?"

"As the King's leading officer in this part of the county, you have as much authority to grant me release upon surety as FitzAllan."

"I'm not sure about that."

"You are still a deputy sheriff, are you not?"

"The last I heard. Although I've a feeling it won't last long after what happened to you."

"In an emergency, a man does what he can to serve the King and to protect those who serve him as well."

"Does one?"

Stephen untied the thong securing the cloth sack. He poured out the silver coins, and counted out a pile containing twenty shillings. "You heard, of course, that I was wanted on a charge of murder. You even thought I had been arrested. But then I presented myself to appear and answer the charge upon an offer of surety. The larger pile is for the surety. The smaller one is for your trouble."

"You expect me to take such a risk for a mere twenty shillings?" Henle's fingers drummed the table. "Tell you what.

You put up that fine warhorse of yours as surety. What's he worth, twenty, thirty pounds? And I'll take care of what lies there."

"Done. But I will have the surety in writing, and a copy sent with an explanatory letter to the Prince."

"You pay for the letter."

"Done again, as long as there is a receipt with the Prince's seal."

Henle smiled without humor. "I can't promise what the Prince will do, but I'll certainly ask."

Stephen scooped half the money back into the cloth he had brought with him. "You can have this when I have my receipt and the copies."

"Just be sure to bring that delightful horse to me. Then you can have your writ."

'Of course. Tomorrow morning suit you?"

"I doubt my scribblers can work faster than that," Henle said with a laugh. "They are a thumb-fingered lot."

Chapter 13

The problem of how to find this troupe of players had weighed on the back of Stephen's mind, and now that he had dealt with the problem of his freedom at least temporarily, it came to the fore.

Stephen was pondering the question as he returned to the castle gate, where Randel, the gate ward, was guarding the realm upon his stool in the passageway, spear propped against the wall beside him. He was one of the older men of the garrison, with a shoulder that drooped due to a wound suffered in fighting with the Welsh.

"Why, sir," Randel said, "you're still loose. What magic did you work with Sir Walter to overcome his hatred of you?"

Stephen checked to see if anyone was looking. He rubbed his fingers together.

"That always works, doesn't it?" Randel laughed.

"Say," Stephen said. "You wouldn't happen to have heard about a troupe of players who recently came to town."

"Why, I have, sir. They came by here asking for a license to play at the castle Saturday and today, but Sir Walter refused them. Thinks they're troublemakers and thieves. He doesn't want to expose his guests to them. So, we sent them to the Pigeon to catch the crowd at bowls."

The Pigeon was an inn operated by one Herbert Jameson at the junction of Linney Lane and Corve Road below the bridge over the River Corve — an inn for a man on a budget without much to offer in terms of a bed or food but otherwise popular with the bowling crowd; it sat on the only flat ground suitable for bowls. At least the grass was mowed so the balls rolled straight and the ale was not sour.

"Still there, you think?" Stephen asked.

"I have no idea, sir, but it wouldn't surprise me. Sunday is Herb's biggest day. There's a good bit of money to be made then, I would imagine."

"Your attention is requested!" Herb Jameson shouted from his place upon one of his garden tables where he had climbed to be seen and heard better. "Your attention is requested!"

"What the devil?" said a fellow at the table over from that occupied by Stephen and Gilbert, which was under the trees lining the river to give them a good vantage point to observe everything that happened in the Pigeon's back garden. "What does Herb want now?"

"Perhaps it's another price increase," commented a companion.

Herb shouted again. The hubbub of conversation dwindled and the bowlers hesitated in their games, except for one fellow whose cast went wide.

"That counts," his opponent said with a grin.

"Does not!" the errant bowler exclaimed. "I was interfered with!"

"Everyone!" Herb announced when he finally got almost everyone's attention. "We have a special treat for you today — straight from that teeming city of London, the Southwark Players!"

"Do you really think they're from Southwark?" asked Gilbert, who had recently been all the way to Southwark and had seen no sign of players there, nor heard talk of any.

"I doubt it," Stephen said. "It sounds good though, eh?"

At Herb's introduction, a drum around the corner of the Pigeon began to beat a lively rhythm accompanied by the melodious trilling of a flute, and the players emerged, some prancing, some performing somersaults, backflips, and handstands; all of them attired in outlandish costumes of green, blue, red, except for the man banging the drum who was dressed as a friar, complete with tonsure, only that was false, a linen cap with horsehair glued to the sides.

One of their number sprang upon Herb's table and performed a handspring and a full somersault in the air on the other side that ended into a full split on the ground: a pretty red-haired girl, thin as a twig. She wore a tight-fitting green outfit with green wings projected from her shoulders.

"That must be her," Gilbert said. "Do you think she's supposed to be an angel? I've never seen one with green wings."

"I think she's meant to be a fairy," Stephen said.

The musicians circulated among the tables, playing furiously, while the acrobats continued to gyrate and dance in an intricate pattern in front of the cleared space before Herb's table. Those who had been occupied by their bowls had by now abandoned the game, and the crowd was packed tight around that space, mouths open in amazement, the atmosphere rent by cascades of applause at this spectacular feat and that.

Stephen was amazed that the performers could keep it up so long, for it must have been quite exhausting. But at last the display halted.

"And now!" cried one of the players, a fellow wearing a headdress of false deer antlers, "Our very own Matilda the Flyer!"

At this announcement, the red-haired girl bowed to the ground.

"So, not Mary after all," Gilbert murmured.

"Apparently."

One may think Matilda was nicknamed the Flyer because of her abilities at vaulting, but that proved not to be the case. Two of the players escorted her to a ladder put up against the Pigeon as if she was a great lady. Matilda climbed to the top of the ladder, where a rope was fastened to the house stretching to one of the trees by the river. A player mounted the ladder after her, and handed up two common hoops like children rolled in the streets.

Matilda stepped upon the rope and, slowly and tentatively, began to walk along it. The spectators fell silent. There was a gasp here and there. But no one dared to say a thing.

Matilda got halfway, then put each arm through one of the hoops, and balancing on one foot, began to twirl the hoops around her outstretched arms.

She started forward again, the hoops twirling, one tentative and wobbling step at a time, until at last, to the crowd's great relief, she reached the end of the rope. She threw aside the hoops, leaped into the air — to shouts of alarm and horror as the crowded expected her to fall to earth and die — and was caught by two of the players who had positioned themselves beneath her unnoticed by anyone, since all attention was on the girl.

The catchers set Matilda on her feet and she raised her hands to thunderous applause, shouts and whistles of approval that probably were heard as far as Bromfield.

Meanwhile, other players circulated through the crowd with hats off to collect contributions from the amazed and grateful spectators.

"Thank you so much!" called the man with the deer antlers. "If you enjoyed this performance, let me remind you that we will be performing again on market day in the High Street! Come one, come all! Bring your wives and children! You'll see death defying feats that make Matilda's walk pale in comparison! And our mummers will perform plays never before seen in Ludlow! Prepare to be astounded, prepared to be amazed, and prepare to be thrilled — but not if you stay home!"

And with that, the players pranced and danced out of sight around the corner of the Pigeon to the beat of the drum and the trilling of the flute.

Monday afternoon, Stephen climbed Broad Street to the guildhall. As was often the case, there were three town bailiffs whiling away the day on benches upon the columned porch of the hall, which was formed by the floor above jutted out from the main part of the building. They stirred themselves when Stephen arrived, and would have risen from their comfortable positions had Stephen not motioned for them to remain seated.

"Good day to you, yer lordship," one of the bailiffs said. "Good to see you out and about. Sorry about that trouble down in Hereford."

"We didn't believe that charge when we heard of it," another said.

"Thanks, boys," Stephen said. "Is Tarbent here?"

"Oh," said the first bailiff, "he's here all right. It's been a day of tantrums. So noisy!"

"Nobody killed, though?" Stephen asked. The reference to tantrums was a sign that Tarbent had taken a cane to one of his copyists.

"Not yet, though the day's young."

"I'll show myself in," Stephen said, although he never expected anyone to stir from that comfortable bench.

Stephen heard Tarbent fuming even before he opened the door.

"Good!" Stephen said as he entered the chamber. "I found you in a good mood! The bailiffs said you had been out of sorts."

"They did?" Tarbent snarled. "They're still down there?" He leaned out the window and shouted, "Get your no-good arses up and go fine somebody!" He turned back and said, "There's enough crime around here to make the town rich, but those lazy bastards can't be bothered to keep order."

"Accounts not balance again?" Stephen asked.

"They would if I didn't have oafs for assistants. None of them could count their fingers on one hand and get to five."

"A sorry state of affairs for a professional such as yourself."

Tarbent regarded Stephen with narrowed eyes. "You want something."

"Well, a small something."

"Spit it out. What is it? Can't you see we're busy here? Running a town is an exhausting business. I can't have my attention diverted by your social visits."

"This isn't exactly a social visit. I expect that band of players has been by here."

"They came Friday. Bought a license to play at the market. Why?"

"There was trouble with them in Hereford. A robbery of a wealthy man. Are you sure it's a good idea to let them into town? If they cause trouble, it will reflect badly on you, now that you know, especially if the victim is connected. People are sure to find out . . . that it was your doing."

Tarbent blinked at the threat. "It's too late for that. They've already paid for their license."

"Revoke the license."

"That means I have to give them their money back."

"Don't tell me you've spent it already."

"No, I haven't spent it already."

"Well?"

Tarbent hemmed and hawed. Perhaps he had already spent the money.

"How much was the license?" Stephen asked.

"A full shilling."

"That's a lot. Is that the ordinary charge?"

"They're bound to make three or four times that, if they're any good."

"I see." Stephen counted out a shilling from the expense money Margaret had given him. "Here's the equal of the license. Now send one of your clerks to tell them that you've changed your mind about it, and give them their money back."

Tarbent's hand hovered over the pile of pennies. He swept them across the table. He found a leather pouch for it. He held out the pouch to a clerk watching in the corner, a bruise on his cheek and pen poised.

"Arnald," Tarbent said, "go tell that bunch staying at the Pigeon that I've reconsidered their license for this week's market."

When Arnald had gone, Tarbent asked, "Why are you doing this? Were you the one robbed?"

"No, an acquaintance was."

"Ah! Why not appeal against them?"

"I do not have satisfactory proof yet. Only suspicions. Which I hope will be proved in due course."

Tarbent wagged a finger. "You are the wily one!"

Stephen went down to the Pigeon at supper time. His mind was filled with anxiety and dread. He had arranged for the troupe to get word of the loss of the license late enough in the day that they could not leave and reach another town by sundown. He thought this would encourage them to stay one more night. All he needed was this one night. Or so he hoped.

The bowling pitch was deserted when Stephen passed through the gate, as he had come out Linney Gate, a small sally port through the north wall of town, and down the steep slope to Linney Lane and thus reached the inn by the back way.

He entered the back door; passed the kitchen, waving to the cooks laboring over the fire where a loin of pork was turning on a spit, smelling very good; and came to the front hall.

Herb turned at his entrance. "Sir Stephen! What brings you here?"

"I'm a bit tired of Edith's food," Stephen said. "The menu never seems to change. I thought I'd try something different."

Herb fell for the lie, since it implied that his food was good enough to compete with Edith's, and he wanted to believe that. "Well, then, let me show you my best table."

Herb escorted Stephen to the table by the front window looking out on Corve Street. It was the best table in summer because of the view and the good light, golden and gentle with the setting sun, the sky clear and blue for a change.

Stephen settled onto a stool as Herb said, "You are lucky today. We have braised pork for the discriminating palate."

"I saw that. I think I will indeed have some."

"I'll bring it straight away, with bread, cheese and boiled cabbage. Or would you prefer the beans? What will you have to drink?"

"Wine, I think. And I don't mind cabbage, as long as you're not stingy with the salt."

"Excellent." Herb hurried to a keg to draw a pitcher of wine.

Only then did Stephen allow his eyes to wander around the room, which was more full of diners than he would have expected. He had been relieved to see when he entered that the troupers were at a corner table. Now he locked eyes for an instant with the red-haired girl, Matilda. Normally when you looked at a pretty girl who was a stranger, she tossed her head and looked away. But Matilda held his gaze. She had the most remarkable blue eyes. He nodded with a slight smile. She looked grave.

Herb brought a pitcher of wine and one of water, poured Stephen a cup, and left for the kitchen. Stephen sipped the wine. It was chalky and needed watering down, hence the pitcher of water. He was glad for that pitcher of water. It might enable him to keep his head for what was to come.

Herb came back shortly with a wooden trencher of sliced pork, bread, and cheese, and a bowl of the cabbage.

Stephen pushed a thick button of the pork onto his spoon and, expecting the worst, tried it. "Herb," he said, "this is very good." And surprisingly that was not a lie. The pork was both tasty and tender, not the least bit overcooked.

While he ate, Stephen kept a surreptitious eye on the troupers in the corner. They appeared to be studying him with the same attempt to be covert about it. Eyes thrown over shoulders swept the room pretending to take in everything in the chamber, but lingered on Stephen before moving off.

When Stephen had cleaned the trencher and the bowl, Herb returned to collect them. Stephen made a display of paying him from a fat purse, even though that was not normally required yet, since he had not finished his wine. The eyes at the troupers table took notice of that purse before Stephen put it back in his belt pouch.

Stephen poured another tiny bit of wine in his cup, though trying to make it appear as if the quantity was much larger than it actually was. He sipped ostentatiously and looked out the window at the mowed fields across the street, where sheep and ravens were grazing on the stubble.

Matilda came to the window not far away and looked out at this pleasant scene, pretending to admire the view.

"I say," Stephen said to her. "Care to join me in a cup?"

Matilda glanced at Stephen as if to dismiss the suggestion. But then she said with some reserve, "Very well, sir."

She sat on the bench opposite him. Stephen fetched a cup from the bar since no servers were about. He poured her cup to brimming and his about a quarter full, adding some water.

He raised his cup. "To your performance yesterday. I saw it. It was quite something."

"Thank you," Matilda said, taking a deep draught. "I saw you there. You were with a little fat man."

"I am surprised you remember me. There were so many."

"You stand out in a crowd."

"I hope that's a compliment."

She smiled.

"I look forward to seeing your performance tomorrow," Stephen said.

That produced an angry look. "Our license has been cancelled. There will be no performance."

"Good Heavens, why?"

"The town has decided we are undesirables, troublemakers."

"I am sorry."

"It happens."

"What will you do now?"

"Go on to Shrewsbury, I suppose."

"The town's loss."

"It certainly is."

"Your loss too, all that money you stood to make."

Matilda's mouth became a thin line. "Yes."

"Your kind must live on the edge, always close to ruin and starvation. Life is hard on the road."

"It is. I am surprised you would entertain the thought."

"I have been on the road. Not as a player, but as a wandering knight. Fortunately, I have come into my manor at last, so those days are behind me."

"You are lucky to be born into a life where such things are possible."

"I suppose that's true." Stephen raised his cup again. "But for the grace of God."

Matilda smiled and drank with Stephen to God's grace, even though it had fallen unevenly upon them.

From there, the conversation wandered into more friendly topics than poverty and ruin, and Stephen was able to make her laugh now and then, and the laugh did not sound forced at all. She had to be as good an actress as she was an acrobat. They drank and talked as the sun set and the night settled on Ludlow.

At last, Stephen put down his cup and stood up, swaying a bit in what he hoped looked convincingly like he had had too much wine.

"I must be off," he said, "before they ring the curfew."

"You live in the town?"

"Yes. I have a house there."

"For someone like you I'd think the curfew doesn't matter."

"Well, it often doesn't, actually."

"An excuse to go, then."

"I've an early day tomorrow."

"I see. And eager to get home to your wife."

"I have no wife now. It's an empty bed to which I return."

"It doesn't have to be empty."

Stephen paused as if considering this. "It doesn't?"

"As long as there is a suitable gift in the morning."

Stephen paused again. "That is a possibility."

He held out a hand. Matilda took it as she rose.

They went out the front door to Corve Street together.

From Linney Lane to the town gate, the houses along Corve Street sat shoulder to shoulder, forming an unbroken wall on either side, except at one or two places. About halfway to the gate on the left, rested a timber house belonging to a certain Mistress Webbere, just before the road curved to the left and the ground began its rise to the summit of the hill on which the town sat. There was an alley at Mistress Webbere's house where a stairway led up to the second-floor room she rented. Stephen knew this house well.

About twenty yards from this alley, Matilda paused and said, "A moment. I have a stone in my shoe."

She bent down and wormed a finger in the top of her shoe.

"There," she said. "Got it."

She rose and took Stephen's right arm.

When they reached the alley, her grip tightened on his right arm with astonishing strength for a woman who appeared so small and frail so that he could not draw his dagger, while the snicking of the footsteps of the men behind them changed abruptly to pounding as they charged forward.

But Stephen did not try for his dagger. Instead, he looped his right arm around and under Matilda's left arm to obtain an underhook, then pushed down on her head and up on the underhook so she flipped onto her back. He punched her hard in the head so, he hoped, she would not interfere with what happened next.

And turned to face his attackers rushing out of the alley.

There were three of them.

They rushed at him spread out, one to take his front and the others to take him on either side. In the dark, he could not see if they were armed, and there was no time to draw his dagger. So, he lunged forward with a left punch that caught the man in front in the face so that his head shot backwards and his feet forward. His body now horizontal to the ground, he went down with a great thud.

Stephen turned to the closest man, the one on his right. He sensed rather than saw the club descending toward his head. He ducked to the left, caught the attacking arm, and punched the fellow in the head, then swept him off his feet, relieving him of the club as he hit the ground.

That left the man on the left.

But then help arrived: Randel, the gate ward, and four of his mates.

Two of the other gate wards tackled the third attacker as he turned to flee. They collapsed in a tangle of thrashing arms and legs. Another warden lifted the man Stephen had knocked out while Randel took on the fellow Stephen had swept off his feet.

Stephen went to Matilda who had got to her hands and knees. He tried to force one arm behind her back. She started to struggle. She had enough strength in her little frame for three men, and he was not able to get her under control until two of the wardens came to his aid. But at last they got her pressed down on her stomach and her arms behind her back so that they could be tied with a leather thong.

"That was more work than I expected," Randel panted when they had all the troupers secured. "I should have charged you more."

"Let's get them to the gaol," Stephen said. "Or will I have to pay for that service separately?"

"No, although I don't think the boys would mind an extra tip, for good service."

"We'll see about that."

Chapter 14

Stephen led Matilda into the guardroom at the castle's main gate. He would have let her sit on a stool, but she continued to worm about as she had done all the way here, so he pushed her down into a corner. He took the stool for himself.

They regarded each other for a long time, Matilda with hatred and Stephen trying to keep his expression as blank as possible.

Randel stuck his head in the room. "The others are all tidy and secure."

"Good," Stephen said. "Can you get another candle? This one may not last long enough." There was half a candle left on a table by the far wall. It should be good for an hour yet, but there was no telling how long the questioning of Matilda would take.

"So, we'll hang then?" Matilda asked at last.

"I expect so. Unless . . ."

"Unless what?"

"I have some questions. If you answer them truthfully, I may reconsider my presentment against you."

"Ha! Fat chance of that! Your sort always lies."

"Be silent and you hang for certain. Answer me, and take a chance that you live."

Matilda's mouth pursed in thought. "You're the one who had our license cancelled."

"I did."

"What made you think we'd try a robbery?"

"You are predictable."

"Come now, you couldn't have known."

Stephen smiled. "I took a chance. It's what you did in Hereford, a robbery on the night before you left. I saw no reason to expect you would change your habit. I imagine that's what you do in every town."

Matilda looked nervous about the mention of Hereford. But she did not deny a robbery there.

"Tell me," Stephen said, "what happened with Rogier FitzHerbert."

"How well do you know Hereford?"

"Well enough."

"Then you probably know about Grope Lane."

"Everyone in the county knows about Grope Lane."

"So, you know it's run by this woman, Squinty Peg."

"I knew she had some influence there."

"Ha! She runs it like a lord. No one takes a shit but she knows about it and gives permission."

"What does this have to do with Sir Rogier?"

"Everything. Things been tight with the band. Hereford's a rich town, but our takings weren't that great. We got expenses, you know? The horses cost a lot in hay, and the boys have tendency to spend too freely. So, I was trying to make a bit of extra change in Grope Lane. Squinty found out about it and sent her boys around to put a stop to it. They would have beat me right good to boot, but she saw I needed money and she had a scheme to get some."

"Money from FitzHerbert? That's bold."

"She had a boy who served him, that Martin. You know about him?"

"We've met, after a fashion."

"Well, then, Martin had let slip that FitzHerbert had a full five pounds in ready coin just lying around in his bedchamber. You'd think it'd be safe there, but Squinty, she's a cunning one. She had a plan. She had me dangle myself in front of Martin and FitzHerbert at that bathhouse down by the river. She said Martin wouldn't fail to resist."

"Why do that?"

"Because Martin had refused to steal the money. He said it was stupid, that it would kill the goose."

"That's what Squinty told you."

"Yeah."

"So, you've dangled yourself."

"Yeah, it was easy. Martin is a horny bastard. He said FitzHerbert likes to watch him do the girls and the boys. So, we went back to FitzHerbert's house."

"So, did you steal the money?"

"Sure."

"How did you manage that? You didn't have them jumped on the road by your two friends, did you, and strong arm them into giving it over?"

"You know about Bill and Hank, do you?"

"They were found, after."

Matilda looked sad. "Yeah, it ended bad."

"We'll get to the ending in due course. How did you pull off the theft?"

"Squinty knew we'd be going back to the house for some fun. She gave me a powder to put in the wine. It put them both to sleep. So, I got the key from around FitzHerbert's neck, where I was told it would be, unlocked the chest and that was that. There, at least."

"Tell me about the ending."

"I came downstairs and left the house through the back door, where Bill and Hank were supposed to be waiting."

"Supposed?"

"Squinty was there with ten of her boys. Bill and Hank were already dead. I only got away because no man alive can hold me or run me down."

"Until tonight."

"Well, there is that. But you were lucky. You'll never get another chance."

"Squinty got the money?"

"Every penny. It was too heavy to carry and get away. Anyway, one of her lads yanked it out of my hands first thing."

"Did you happen to notice a letter in the chest with the money?" he asked.

"Yeah, I recollect something like that. It was right on top. A pair of them, in fact."

"Did you take them, too?"

"Nah, I wasn't interested in no letters."

"So, why was it necessary to kill them?"

"Kill who?"

"Martin and FitzHerbert."

Matilda's mouth opened in surprise. "They're dead?"

"Martin was found strangled in bed and FitzHerbert an apparent suicide. But I don't think it was suicide."

"They were alive when I left them, snoring like babies."

"You believe her, then," Gilbert said, doubt in his voice. His eyes were sunken holes due to the shadows cast by the single low candle on Stephen's favorite table in the Broken Shield.

"It's always a mistake to trust a woman," Harry said. "She'll lead you astray for the fun of it." He said this with a smile and a glance at Joan. "Ain't that right, my dear?"

"I do expect you to do as you're told," Joan said. "Sometimes a little white lie is necessary for that purpose."

"I do believe her, I think," Stephen said. He puffed at the flame to make it dance. "Her story is easily checked. Besides, if Matilda got any money from the robbery, she'd have had no need to attack me."

"What," Harry said, "you're just going to walk up to Squinty Peg and say, and oh, about that robbery at the FitzHerbert house, did you have a hand in that? And what about those two murders after? How long do you think you'll last if you do that?"

"About two heart beats," Gilbert said. "Then her boys will fall on you, truss you up, and deliver you to FitzAllan. I doubt he'll be much concerned about your pledge of surety."

"What else can I do?" Stephen asked. "This path is a dead end."

"Looks like I'll have to do it," Harry said. "There's too much chance that Stephen will be recognized. And either of you will just muck it up, anyway."

"You!" Joan exclaimed.

"Sure," Harry said. "I know Grope Lane. Been there more than once. Know Peg as well from years back. No one will think a thing if I thump through there with my ear to the ground."

"Well, you're not going alone," Joan said. "You can no more protect yourself if things go wrong than a puppy."

"I don't know about that," Stephen said, remembering a night last year when Harry had killed a man who had come to assassinate Stephen in Gilbert's stable. "He's a man of surprises."

"Nonetheless, he isn't going alone," Joan declared.

"It's a good idea not to argue with her," Harry said. "You'll just lose. Pretend as if it's your idea. That's what I intend to do. My dear, I could use your help on this perilous mission. Would you care to assist me?"

"Good boy," Joan said, patting Harry on the head.

"See?" Harry asked the others. "She is damp clay in my hands."

Chapter 15

Getting Harry to Hereford took much of the following day. The last time he made the journey, he had gone tied to a saddle, but now he had a cart of his own. However, the pony pulling the cart couldn't keep up with Stephen's horse and Gilbert's mule for long at a trot. Stephen chaffed at the delay, but it couldn't be helped.

It was late afternoon when they turned into the yard at the Trumpet Inn. It was a finely made building with timbers freshly painted blue and the whitewash between them scrubbed of mold so that the walls fairly shone. Harry had seen it from the road but never from the inside, for it was too expensive an establishment for the likes of him, even when he had had his legs, since he had been a farmer and day laborer who had done any odd job someone would pay for. He would like to enjoy its comforts, but perhaps he'd have the opportunity that night.

"Joan," he said, "fetch my rags."

"They're right beside you," Joan said, rising on the bed of the cart to get the kinks out of her legs. She then hopped down.

Harry dug into the linen satchel that had rested behind them in the cart and fished for his rags. Since he had become a man of means and left the vocation of beggar behind, he had bought a new shirt, coat and stockings, which he had tailored to the length of his stumps. A good suit of clothes was something to be savored, for clothes were the mark of a man. He regretted that he would have to put on his rags again. Yet it was a good thing he had saved them — he had done that because he had not been confident that his new-found affluence would last. And perhaps it would fail yet. Fate was fickle and cruel.

He threw the blanket they had brought over his head, and struggled out of his good clothes and into his shabby ones beneath its cover.

"Ah, so handsome," Gilbert said, when Harry shed his blanket. "The Harry we knew and disapproved of has not entirely disappeared."

Harry mussed his hair, crossed his eyes, and stuck out his tongue.

Stephen leaned over the railing to try and catch the tongue. Harry batted the reaching hand away.

"You'll need quite a bit of dirt as well," Stephen said. "Dirt used to follow him like a cloud," Stephen added for Joan's benefit.

"Pay no attention to this slander," Harry said. "Let's be off to Grope Lane while there's still daylight."

Joan grasped the pony's bridle and led the cart into the street.

"That way," Harry said, gesturing toward Wydemarsh Gate as he clutched the blanket about himself to conceal his rags.

"I know that way," Joan said. "I'm not stupid."

"Just making sure. I don't want to get lost."

They had to pay a toll to get in, of course, and it was higher than if they had been on foot, owing to the pony and cart, which were charged extra.

One of the gate wards looked over Harry, who clutched the blanket about himself, and asked, "What's the matter with him? I hope he don't got the plague or something."

"Just a fever," Joan said, as if it was nothing of consequence."

But the ward backed up anyway and made Joan put the coins for the toll on his stool.

"Off you go," the ward said and motioned them to pass.

"I wish I could give him a sickness," Harry said darkly. "So rude."

"Oh, hush. You're lucky he let us in at all, what with suspecting you're sick."

Watching through a gap in the blanket, Harry directed Joan where to go, since she had never been to Hereford. They took the first left onto Malieres Street, which further on became Jews Street. Harry's sister's house came up on the right, and he almost called out for Joan to stop. He had visited here in the spring, and had probably worn out his welcome then, but he still yearned to stop. She had not been his favorite sister, but they had got on better when they were both grown. The temptation to linger would have been too great, so he said nothing to Joan as they went by the house and the street met the wall to curve around to Bye Street at the gate.

"Where to?" Joan asked, for Bye Street and another one, Olde Street, met at a wide place before the gate.

"Pass over Bye Street and turn right on the next one," Harry said. "Grope Lane is the first left up ahead just before the market."

At long last, they reached Grope Lane.

"You can stop here," Harry said, when they were three houses from the corner. He threw off the blanket and tossed his begging platform, a board of planks nailed to two rockers, out of the back of the cart.

"What are you doing?" Joan asked.

"I'm getting out."

"Why? We're almost there."

Harry pulled on his heavy leather gloves which protected his fists as he propelled himself along on the board. "I'm going on alone."

"No, you aren't."

Harry grasped Joan's arm and pulled her to her knees. He was so strong that she could not resist, even though she had enough wiry strength to defy most men.

"There are really bad people in there," he said. "Grope Lane is no place for a pretty young woman like you. If you have no one to protect you, there's every chance you'll be taken and ill used. And you know what that's like."

"I can protect myself."

"You may think so, but I will not take the chance. I don't want the failure to be on my conscience."

"What if something happens to you?"

"It well could, but it's less likely it will be fatal. I'll just get robbed."

"You're making a mistake."

"No, I'm not, and you know it."

Harry finished buckling himself onto his board, and swung toward the corner with seemingly easy strokes of his massive arms. He had been strong before his accident, but the need to get around using only his arms and shoulders had given him great ones.

"Go back to the inn," he said over his shoulder. "Come back at sundown and fetch me here."

Grope Lane had not changed. The houses were as dingy as Harry remembered, the paint and plaster flaking off, laundry hanging from the upper windows, the street rutted and full of holes which were troublesome in daylight and a trap at night. The stone piss tank on the corner was overflowing into the dirt as usual. A mangy dog snarled at him from a doorstep. A whore in an upstairs window spotted him, pointed, and said something to a person behind her: another whore who came to the window. They hooted at him, as people often did when they first saw Harry. A black cat dashed across the street from one narrow gap between the houses to another. People stopped to make the sign of the Cross, for black cats were unlucky. Someone batted Harry on the back of the head as he went by: a couple of boys who danced about shouting insults at him. Harry ignored them and kept going. After a time, the boys got bored and went away.

Harry thumped along as best he could, pausing now and then to hold out his begging bowl and cry for alms. No one stopped to give charity, but that was not unusual. He often went for hours without earning anything. Begging was hard work and required persistence and perseverance.

He got about a third of the way down, where a lane ran north between two houses to an orchard. He swung to the side across the street from Squinty Peg's house, which stood by the lane, or what had been her house. Harry wondered if it still was. He got off the board, stripped off his gloves, and went to work proper, calling out to every passerby.

It wasn't long before a bailiff and a tough-looking stocky man of about twenty with bad pimple scars on his cheeks and a blue cloth cap stopped before him.

"What're you think you're doing here?" asked the man in the cloth cap.

"What does it look like, you dumb shit?" Harry responded. "I'm working the street."

The man in the blue cap bent down to grasp Harry's collar, but Harry got hold of him first. The man in the blue cap was strong, but Harry was far stronger.

"What the —" cried the man in the blue cap as Harry released him.

"Don't get rough with me, Snotty," Harry said, remembering the man's nickname from years before when he was a day laborer and before he got his farm, which he had lost along with his wife and children after the accident that cost him his legs. "You'll just get hurt."

The bailiff, who had observed this without expression, asked, "You got a license?"

"Sure do," Harry said. He pulled the vellum from where it had been under his belt.

The bailiff examined the license. "Looks in order," he said to Snotty.

"Well, no one's allowed on the lane without mum's permission," Snotty said. "And he ain't got it."

"That's between him and her," the bailiff said, returning the beggar's license, which Harry had acquired during his spring visit. "I got nothing further to do with it."

"Yer paid to!"

"I'm thirsty," the bailiff said. He turned away and strolled off.

"So what you gonna do now, Snotty?" Harry asked. "Call out your brothers to do the work you're not man enough to do yourself? It will take the lot of them, even though I'm not the man I used to be."

Snotty was so furious by now that his mouth worked but he was unable to produce more than grunts and babble, spittle flying from his lips. And the end, he could not contain his fury. He kicked at Harry's head. But Harry caught the foot and, pressing down on the knee, dropped Snotty hard on his back.

"How's yer mum doing, by the way?" Harry asked as Snotty climbed to his feet, fuming. "It's been a long time since I've seen her."

"You know mum?" Snotty asked, suspiciously.

"Course. You remember, I had a bit of business with her now and then. Maybe she'll come out and have a chat for old time's sake. I know something she might like to hear."

"What the fuck could you possibly know that she might be interested in?"

"It's about that business last week at the FitzHerbert house."

"What business?" Snotty asked but not in a way that was convincing of his ignorance.

"Come on, Snotty, the thing involving that girl player. I bet you were in on it, not that I care any. Have a go. Tell Squinty that Harry from Richard's Castle is outside."

At the mention of the girl player, Snotty grew visibly alarmed. "You're Harry?"

"What's left of me."

"Don't look like you at all."

"Well, what's it been, twelve, fifteen years? You were a little tike last I saw you, running wild and cutting people's purses."

"All right. Don't run away, now." Snotty chuckled at his joke and went into the house across the street.

Some time passed before Squinty Peg appeared in the doorway. She strode across the road, cane in hand, a fashion item that she carried even when Harry had known her, although it was more weapon than means of support.

"You don't look like the Harry I knew," Squinty said when she stood over him.

"I was taller then," Harry said. "And better dressed."

Squinty bent down and took Harry's chin in her hand. She turned his head right and left. She let go and stood up. "You seem to be him, all right. What's Theo up to these days?"

"Don't know. Came straight here."

"About that. We heard you were begging up in Ludlow. It's a long way from here. What could bring you so far?"

"You might want to hear this, quiet like. Not on the street where anyone might hear."

"Good idea."

Squinty marched back to her house.

"So," Squinty asked when they were seated at her hall table, "how did you get here? It's a long way to crawl."

"I have a girlfriend," Harry said. "She has a cart."

"You!" Snotty scoffed. "With a girl!"

"My wand is longer than my legs. It's the envy of Ludlow. The girls fight over it."

Squinty laughed. "That's the Harry I remember. So, tell me what brought you here."

"An overheard conversation."

"Go on."

"I have my little hideaway, see, a stall in the stable of this inn. The owner rents to me. A troupe of players came to town last Friday. I heard them talking in the stable early Saturday while I was savoring the dawn in my stall. Your name came up."

"Not in a friendly way, I am assuming."

"No, not at all. Seems this girl and a couple of others had a spot of trouble involving you and some sort of robbery at some rich man's house."

"Go on."

"Well, I didn't get all of the details, 'cause they talked so low. Seems they were put up to the robbery by you, and once they pulled it off, you had two of the lads killed and took all the money. The girl got away. She was sweet on one of the lads, a fellow named Bill, and was furious you'd knifed him."

"So?"

"This Bill was from London. His brother is high up in one of the gangs there. She swore she'd tell the brother and have him send someone to kill you. You know how it is, you can't let such a harm to family pass unavenged."

Squinty stroked her chin. "No, you can't."

"There is one other thing," Harry said.

"What?" asked Squinty.

"There's this fellow in Ludlow, used to be the coroner there."

"Attebrook." She smiled. "Got arrested for murder, and somehow escaped from the castle gaol. No one can figure out how he managed it, but I think it had to be an inside job. Your brother, Theo, have anything to do with it? He works at the castle."

"Theo's gone straight as an arrow since he married Sarah. You know that."

"I'm not so sure. I keep hearing things. So, what's Attebrook have to do with any of this?"

"The rich man's steward hired him to find a letter that went missing the day of the robbery. I'm sure he'll pay a lot of money to get it back."

"Who, the steward or Attebrook?"

"Either one, I'll bet, although I think you're going to have trouble finding Attebrook. You don't happen to know where the letter is?"

"No, regrettably I don't. What's in this letter?"

"I'm not sure. But it's got to be important."

"How do you know about it?"

"The innkeeper's his assistant."

"I suppose you expect to be paid for this."

"Come on, Squinty. Knowing you've got to watch your back from now on has to be worth something."

Squinty was quiet for a long time. At last she said, "I suppose it is, my friend."

She produced three pennies from her purse. "That should do it, don't you think?"

Three full pennies were three days' wages for the working man and could buy a gallon of wine, if Harry had been inclined in that direction. In the relative scheme of things, it was decent payment for his work.

Harry plucked up the pennies. "Thanks, Squinty. Nice doing business with you."

"Take care of yourself, Harry."

There was no point in lingering in Grope Lane, so Harry dragged himself back to the corner. Two hours of daylight remained, and the market to the left by Saint Peter's Church was still underway, although it had to be winding down. Still, the chance of making a little more money should not be wasted. So, Harry clumped down as far as he dared on Olde Street. He did not go into the market proper, but stayed just beyond its periphery. Begging markets required a special license, which he did not have.

Harry set his bowl on the ground before him and called out, "Alms! Alms for a poor soldier hurt in the wars!" After an hour, when this produced little result, he changed to, "See the horror of a poor man's degradation!" which was accompanied by a peek at his stumps. Those wishing a better view had to pay for the privilege, and this proved to be a more lucrative appeal.

One of those who could be expected to come forward for a view of his stumps was a boy of about twelve or thirteen whom Harry had noticed lingering on the other side of the street. Normally, a boy this age had a job, but this fellow seemed to have nothing to do but pick his nose and leer at the women passing by. The boy also threw glances in Harry's direction whenever he whisked the blanket away from what remained of his legs. Yet he made no move to cross the street for a closer look. It might be that he had no money; a not unusual state of affairs. But then he would still have crowded closer to ride on someone else's contribution.

The more Harry watched the boy, the more he seemed familiar. It took time to figure out why. It was the boy's rather frog-like face: the low forehead, the piggy eyes, and the broad chin. It brought to mind Squinty Peg's face. Now, Squinty Peg's power and influence stemmed in large part from the enormous brood of children that she had dropped upon the world, even though she had not bothered with a husband. Say what you would about them, but they were loyal to her and the family to a fault. Was this boy one of her litter?

A half hour before sundown, Joan returned with the pony cart. She threw Harry's board in the back, while he pulled himself up. She sat down beside him, snapped the reins, and turned the cart around with smoothness and expertise that Harry could only admire.

Now and then, as the cart passed through the market, came around the Guildhall, and turned down Wydemarsh Street, Harry found some excuse to turn about and look back. Frog Boy was following along, pretending to look into shop fronts.

"What are you doing?" Joan asked after a time.

"Keeping watch. We're being followed."

"What on earth?"

"I think it's one of Squinty Peg's brood."

"Why would she have you followed? Did you say something?"

"I don't know, but it can't be good. Squinty's nobody's fool. She never does anything without good reason."

Frog Boy remained behind them after they passed through the gate.

Joan was about to turn into the Turtle's yard, but Harry said, "Go a bit farther."

"Where to? We're almost in the country."

"There's another inn just ahead on the right. See the sign — that yellow stag? Turn in there."

This inn was not as fancy as the Turtle, but it had a stable. A groom emerged from it upon their arrival.

"Will you be staying the night?" the groom asked.

"I don't know about us, but the horse will," Harry said. He gave the groom a half penny and ducked under the blanket to change into his better clothes. The cart lurched downward so that Harry almost tumbled out as the groom unhitched the pony. Then it came up again as Joan pulled the cart toward the inn's side door.

"There you go," Joan said, laying down the traces with more care than the groom had done. "A hop, skip, and a jump."

"Is he still there?" Harry asked, glancing toward the gate. "We should take shelter in the stable and not the inn."

"Afraid that someone will be nasty to you?"

"Beggars don't go into inns."

"But you got your good clothes on now."

"The lad still thinks I'm a beggar," Harry said. "If he sees I went into the inn, Squinty will know I lied, and that something's up."

"Doesn't she guess that already?"

"Probably, but let's not fuel her doubts."

Joan picked up the traces and hauled the cart back to the doorway to the stable.

"Now what?" Joan asked.

"I need to talk to Stephen."

"You could have done that at the Turtle. We went by it."

"I didn't want to lead Squinty's boy there. If Squinty finds out Stephen's in the neighborhood, he's done for. Stephen's a match for the bailiffs, but Squinty's boys are really tough. And there are lots of them. They don't call her the Queen of Grope Lane for nothing."

Chapter 16

Joan did not reach the Turtle Inn until after dark, since Harry would not let her leave until night had fallen for fear of being seen by the boy in the lane. There was no telling if he had remained there, but Harry wasn't taking any chances.

Stephen and Gilbert were still in the hall when Joan entered through the door to the kitchen. Joan looked tired and her feet and the hem of her shift were muddy.

"Did you get supper?" Stephen asked.

Joan nodded.

"Where's Harry?" Gilbert asked.

"At another inn down the road," Joan said.

"Whatever for?" Gilbert asked.

"One of Squinty's lads followed us from Grope Lane. Harry didn't want to lead him here, in case she finds out Stephen's here."

"I am astonished Harry would be so thoughtful," Gilbert said. "FitzAllan might be willing to pay a high price to get ahold of him again."

"You don't give Harry near enough credit," Joan said.

"He does have a certain low cunning," Gilbert said. "I will concede that."

"What did Harry find out?" Stephen asked.

"I think he should tell you himself," Joan said.

Stephen stood up. "We may as well hear his news straightaway."

They left the inn through the kitchen door, crossed the back garden, and hopped the fence at a tumbledown place Joan had discovered on her way in. Strictly speaking, crossing behind the gardens of the houses along the road was a trespass in this field, which was a crime punishable by a substantial fine. But it was doubtful anyone would spot them in the dark if they crept along like ferrets.

Except that Gilbert made quite a bit of noise, huffing, stumbling, and muttering.

"Can you bumble about a bit more quietly?" Stephen asked, exasperated and anxious at the possibility of discovery.

All it would take is someone hearing the commotion through an open rear window to call out. They would be assumed to be up to no good, burglary at best and robbery or murder at worst. And before you knew it the neighborhood would be after them.

"I am doing the best I can," Gilbert protested as he picked himself up again after having tripped on an object invisible in the moonless dark.

"For God's sake, you can be heard all the way to Hereford."

"My life, unlike yours, provided me with little preparation for sneaking about in the dark."

"You should have stayed behind, then."

"But only I will be able to tease the most important threads of information from what Harry has to tell. You can't do it on your own."

"Next thing you'll say is that I can't pee without help."

"No, only Harry might say that."

"Here you go," Joan said as she helped him to his feet. She did not let go and guided him along a thin path bordering the field that took a cat's eyes to detect.

"Thank you, my dear," Gilbert said.

But then Joan stuck out a foot and tripped him.

"Good Heavens!" Gilbert declared. "Why did you do that?"

"Don't speak ill of Harry again," Joan said. "I won't have it."

"You'll have to get used to that around here," Stephen said. "It's our only defense against him. Strike first and often, that is our motto."

"I don't understand you people," Joan said. "I thought you were friends."

"We are friends," Gilbert said. "That is the root of the problem."

Presently the houses ended and open fields and a road faintly visible as a white strip lined with trees stretched into the murky distance. It was quiet except for the singing of crickets and Gilbert's labored breathing.

Stephen crossed the road into the field beyond and started down the backside of the houses on the east side of the road. He had a vague recollection that the inn in question was the third house from the end, but he wasn't sure, and it would not do to blunder into someone's house.

"One house farther, I think," Joan said when Stephen stopped at the third house.

"This is it," Joan added when they reached the back garden of the fourth house.

"How can you tell?" Stephen asked, for in the dark all the houses looked the same.

"That scarf," Joan said, pointing to a scarf hanging from one of the fence posts. "I left it there to mark the way."

"Clever girl," Gilbert said.

Joan retrieved her scarf as the others hopped the fence and crossed the back yard to the stable, which stood on the left of the house just beyond a small apple orchard.

Stephen reached the edge of the orchard when someone came around the side of the stable. An impulse made Stephen grasp Gilbert's shoulder and put a finger to his mouth. They stood among the trees, frozen on the spot with Joan right behind them who had sense enough to do the same without being warned.

The figure urinated against the wall, looked up at the bright stars showing between scudding clouds and went around the corner.

Perhaps it was nothing. Perhaps it was a groom tending to the horses of some late arrival. But something urged Stephen to be cautious, although he could not put a finger on what prompted suspicion.

He slipped around a hay pile with the same care used when stalking deer in the forest to the corner of the stable. He could hear the voices of two men not far away, talking quietly as if they did not want to be overheard. Stephen dropped to a knee and peeked around the corner. The men's silhouettes were visible at the doorway to the stable. They were just standing there, doing nothing. Then they moved a bit, pacing about. Both were carrying short staves.

There was no good reason for men armed like that to be out in the night.

Then he heard a faint groan from within the stable. A third man said, "I said, tell me where that fucker is!" Followed by a squelching sound, like a blow striking home.

The groan had to come from Harry.

Anger flared in Stephen's heart as it sometimes did in moments like this. He tried to control his breathing, to slow himself down, to consider what was the prudent thing to do, as he stood up. The toe of his good foot bumped an object in the grass. Stephen bent down and retrieved the object: a broken ax handle.

Without any further thought, he strode around the corner and marched toward the two men in the doorway.

They turned toward him, startled at his approach. But he was on them in three long strides and on the fourth launched a great blow with the ax handle that connected with one man's neck below the ear. That fellow dropped like a felled ox, and Stephen swung for the next man. His back swing rose from the ground and caught the second fellow under the chin and he went over backward.

Stephen turned toward the doorway, for there was at least one man in there, and perhaps many others. The fury that had sparked his attack had dissipated and now he was in the grip of battle calm, where he seemed to float apart from himself and was aware of every star in the sky, every blade of grass and clod of dirt about him.

The man inside rushed out, bent low, and tackled Stephen, driving him backward. But Stephen had been taken like this before and knew what to do. The trick was not to fight the tackle but to go with it. He grasped his assailant about the waist, rolled backward, and the other man went flying.

Stephen shot to his feet as the third man came at him again. Even in the darkness, brilliant starlight the only illumination, it was apparent he was a big man with massive shoulders — no wonder he had given Stephen such a jolt during his rush.

The third man shot a hard punch at Stephen's head. Stephen slipped to his right, caught the arm, turned, and threw the third man over his shoulder with a flying mare.

The third man landed with a thump at Stephen's feet, and before he could recover or do anything else, Stephen slammed him with his fist two, three, four, five times, until Gilbert grasped his arm and said, "Stop! You'll kill him."

"It's what he deserves," Stephen panted. "Joan, go see to Harry. I think he's hurt. Gilbert, truss up those other two. I'll take care of this one."

Stephen tied the third man with a length of cloth cut from the man's shirt, then rolled him on his back.

By this time the third man was coming around.

The fellow sputtered and might have called out, but Stephen put a hand over his mouth and the point of his dagger under the chin.

"Make any further disturbance, and I'll cut out your tongue," Stephen said. "Understand?"

The fellow nodded.

Stephen removed his hand but not the dagger. "You one of Squinty Peg's boys?"

"Yeah."

"What are you doing here?"

There was some hesitation. Stephen prodded with the dagger.

"Looking for you," the fellow answered. "I assume you're Attebrook. We heard you could fight like the devil."

"Why are you looking for me?"

"Mum wants you dead."

"She'll have to do better than to send the likes of you after me."

"There's plenty more of us, don't worry about that. Enough to turn you into a meat pie. So what you going to do now?"

"That may depend on what shape my friend Harry is in."

"We just knocked him around a bit. Tried to get out of him where you were."

"He say anything?"

"Nah. He's a tough little fucker."

"He wasn't so little once. So, tell me, why does Peg want me dead?"

"She doesn't want anyone connecting us with that business at FitzHerbert's. She knows you're looking into it, been asking questions."

"You mean the robbery involving that player girl, Matilda."

"Yeah."

"Were you there?"

More hesitation, another prod from the dagger.

"Yeah."

"Was the plan only to get the money? Not to kill FitzHerbert and his boy, Martin?"

"We wouldn'ta hurt Martin. He was one of us. Except he wouldn't play over the money."

"Matilda told me Martin and FitzHerbert were alive when she left them."

"That was the plan. Drug 'em and take the stuff. Sweet and simple."

"And did Matilda bring down a letter as well?"

"I don't know anything about no letter."

Stephen tapped the third man on the cheek with the flat of the dagger. "You can go back and tell your mum that I'm not interested in the robbery or what happened to those two player friends of Matilda's. That's Mapuleye's business, not mine. I'm interested in who killed FitzHerbert and Martin, and this letter. I need to talk to her. There are questions about Martin's death I think she may be able to answer. If she's

133

willing, have her come to Saint Owen's Church at noon. Got that?"

"I got it."

Gilbert and Joan dragged Harry out of the stable. It was hard to assess his injuries in the dark by starlight, but he was groaning and not fully conscious. He needed immediate attention, and since it did not seem safe to take him back to the Turtle, Stephen pounded on the door to the inn.

After some time, a voice called from beyond the door, "All right! All right! What is it?"

"Travelers," Stephen said. "We need lodgings."

"No one travels at night, sir! Be gone!"

"If you don't open the door, I'll break it down."

"I should like to see you try!"

"Why does it always involve threats?" Gilbert asked.

"Because they work?" Stephen replied.

"We have a wounded man here who needs immediate attention," Gilbert called to the voice beyond the door. "We've been attacked by Squinty Peg's gang."

"Squinty Peg?" the voice called back. "I want no business with anyone involved with Squinty Peg!"

"We'll pay double," Gilbert said.

There was a thud of a bar being set aside, and the door opened.

"How many are you?" the voice asked.

"Four," Stephen said. He picked Harry up and pushed into the hall of the inn, his back trembling at the effort, for Harry was as solid and heavy as a block of stone. The others entered after him.

Stephen lay Harry on a table. "Get me a light," he ordered. "And some ale. And bar the door. Squinty's boys aren't all gone. And more may show up at any time."

"Dear God!" the innkeeper said. "What sort of trouble are you in?"

"Avoiding murder," Stephen said.

"Squinty is known for that," the innkeeper said. "I'll be right back."

He hurried off and came back with a tallow candle. He also brought ale, a bowl of water and some linen for bandages.

Gilbert kept watch out a window while Stephen and Joan examined Harry. There was matted blood in his hair and a cut beneath on the scalp. His face was already bruised and swelling, an eye shut with another bloody cut on the eyebrow, but he still had all his teeth. In addition, he had bruises on his arms from where he had apparently tried to defend himself.

Stephen propped up Harry's head and fed him some of the ale. He began to come around as Stephen mopped his battered face with a strip of wet linen. This meant more groaning until Stephen sat him upright.

"How did you get here? And where is here?" Harry asked, his words slurred by swollen lips.

"This is …?" Stephen looked at the innkeeper for guidance.

"The Golden Stag," the innkeeper said.

"The Golden Stag," Stephen said. "You sent for us. Something about it not being safe to return to the Turtle."

"Oh, yes, I did," Harry said. "I was wondering what it was like inside here. Not the hovel I expected."

"Thank you," the innkeeper said. "We strive for quality and comfort."

"Your stable needs a little work," Harry said.

"Those who cannot afford a bed never complain about our fresh hay," the innkeeper said.

"You saw Squinty, I take it?" Stephen asked.

"You don't give a man time to collect his wits, do you," Harry said.

"Since you only have half the wits of a normal man, I thought you'd done so already."

"It's the bump on the head. I'm still groggy. But yes, we spoke."

"She denied knowing about the letter and being involved in FitzHerbert's murder?"

"Well, that was the gist. How did you know?"

"We spoke with one of her boys, one of those who thumped you." Stephen jerked a thumb toward the yard. "He said the same thing."

"Why did I bother risking my life then? We could have just caught one and put the thumbscrews on him."

"Stephen prefers the dagger to the throat," Gilbert said from the window. "And I've heard him mutter something about cutting out tongues."

"A man with no subtly, no art," Harry muttered. "Not to mention no sense. Cut out their tongues and they can't tell you what you want to know. I could do his job better than he, and without the bloodshed that follows him around like a bad reputation."

"The catching is the hard part," Stephen said. "We needed bait."

"That's what I am? Bait?"

"And such good bait. A fellow like you can't run away and spoil things. Although I have to confess I did not intend it to turn out so."

"Just my bad luck."

"There are people in the yard," Gilbert said, maintaining his vigil at a crack in one of the window shutters. "Quite a few of them."

"What are they doing?" Stephen asked.

"Collecting their wounded and, from the look of things, discussing what to do next," Gilbert said. "Ah, what do you know? They're leaving."

Stephen blew out the lamp and dashed to the window to see for himself. He saw the dark silhouettes of a dozen or more men as they filed out of the yard.

"Now," the innkeeper said, "about my money."

"Pay the man, Gilbert," Stephen said, slipping out the door. "And don't go back to the Turtle."

136

Chapter 17

"What the —!" Gilbert sputtered.

But Stephen did not hear the rest of Gilbert's protest, for he was jogging across the yard to the far corner of the stable, where he had seen the dark silhouettes vanish.

He peered around the corner. The last of Squinty's boys was climbing over the wicker fence separating the inn's back garden from the field, and making a mess of it from the crackling sounds and the cursing.

Stephen gave them a moment to get ahead, then crossed the yard and eased over the fence without all the racket the men had made.

Beyond the fence was a strip of grass high as a man's thigh. Even in the dark Stephen could see where it had been trampled down by the passage of the men he was following. Beyond the strip of grass was a path, a white swath in the starlight, and beyond that the field itself. Nothing grew there but stubble, for it had been in corn of some type, probably rye or barley, which had been harvested.

Stephen knelt and then lay on his stomach to silhouette the men against the sky. They were some distance ahead. He rose, and followed them. He could not see them well but he could hear them.

This field was owned by FitzHerbert, or more properly was part of his honor and now owned by his heir, a small child too young to own anything. Stephen crept along doing his best to imitate a cat. The FitzHerbert manor house emerged from the darkness as a dark block rising above apple trees planted in the field behind it.

Squinty's gang pressed on through the orchard that lay to the east of the house, but when they struck the fence separating it from the field, they followed the fence.

Stephen kept after them, expecting someone to look back and call out, but no one did.

Shortly, they reached a road which had to be Carts Lane, and turned east. Carts Lane emptied into Frog Lane and the gang turned south. Frog Lane in turn ended at Bye Street.

Stephen thought the gang would cross the road and take to the fields on the other side, but instead, they turned toward Bye Gate, which was only a hundred yards away.

For a moment, Stephen, hanging back in the doorway of a house, thought with incredulity that Squinty's boys just might knock on the gate and ask for admission.

But instead, they turned onto the path that ran along the town ditch.

About a hundred yards on, the Squinty boys crossed the ditch. Stephen slunk close and lay on his stomach behind a patch of tall grass to watch the last of them. There was water flowing in the ditch from the stream on the west side of town that had been diverted for that purpose, and Stephen knew the ditch to be at least armpit deep along its entire length. But the boys sank no farther than knee deep.

Once they crossed the ditch, they seemed to disappear into the side of the slope on the other side.

Stephen waited until it was quiet. He went forward on hands and knees and slid down the steep side of the ditch to the place where the others had crossed. He thrust a hand into to the water and felt around and, as he expected, there was a stone beneath the surface. He stood up and stepped onto the stone. A probing foot found another one. He stepped on that and probed for his companion, and in this careful way crossed the four feet of stream without getting wet above the knees.

Now to figure out where the gang had gone. About three feet from the top of the far slope at the spot they seem to have disappeared, Stephen found a clump of ivy. When he felt within the ivy, his fingers detected a wicker structure supporting it. He pulled up the ivy and the wicker, and discovered that it was a door, covered in the ivy, that concealed the entrance to a tunnel.

He heard faint voices coming from within the tunnel, and made out someone saying, "Hurry up, you bastards. I gotta pee," and receiving the reply, "Put a clamp in it, Alfie."

Stephen had wondered how Squinty's boys had got into and out of the town without having to bother the gate wardens. This was it.

Feeling satisfied in a job well done, Stephen re-crossed the ditch.

Stephen's party left the Golden Stag at dawn and went up the Leominster road to the Dominican monastery. The monks had recently opened a hospital there, and let out space in the nearby barn for relatives of the sick and travelers who could not afford the inns nearer town. The accommodations were rough, consisting only of a spot of hay for a mattress that had its share of fleas and poor ale. Yet it did good business and was often full or nearly so during the summer. Fortunately, there was a shed for the overflow but occupants had to share it with pigs and goats.

It was some way to Saint Owen's Church from there as there was no direct route that did not take one in sight of the city wall, so Stephen rode out well before the appointed time over Gilbert's protests that this meeting was dangerous and should be avoided. Stephen rode northeast, and then took a narrow cart track to the southeast which eventually struck the road leading out of Saint Owen's Gate about a mile from town.

The church occupied the center of the road about sixty yards from the city gate. The midday service had not yet begun when Stephen reached the church, and he tethered his horse to a ring on the wall of a tavern and went in. The table he took by the window offered a good view to the gate, and the window was big enough that he'd be able to leap through it, retrieve his horse, and be away if any trouble appeared, like more of Squinty's gang or sheriff's deputies.

The bell rang for Sext after Stephen had got halfway through the pitcher of ale he had ordered with his dinner of bacon, beans, and bread.

People began leaving the shops along the street and streamed to the church for the service, which was timed to cap their dinner break so they wouldn't lose much work time.

"You're not going?" the taverns proprietor asked Stephen as he prepared to leave.

"No, I don't think so."

This irritated the proprietor, for he apparently expected to close up. He had to direct one of the serving girls to remain to watch over Stephen in case he intended to steal anything. Even well-dressed gentlemen were not above a little light-fingered pilfering, as any tavern and innkeeper knew well. The serving girl plopped on a stool, put her head down on the table, and went to sleep moments after the proprietor and his wife marched out the door.

She was still asleep when the service ended and the church emptied. Stephen crossed the hall and shook the serving girl on the shoulder.

"Time to wake up," he said. "Service is over. They'll be here soon."

She sat up and blinked. "Oh, thanks. You want anything?"

"No, I'm fine."

Stephen returned to his bench by the window.

Presently, Squinty Peg appeared at the city gate. She had words with the wardens in the passage. They all laughed at some joke. Then she hobbled across the bridge over the moat and approached the church, making use of her cane.

She stopped at the church's western and main entrance and looked around. Then she went in.

Stephen paid his bill, belted on his sword, collected his horse, and crossed the street to the church.

Saint Owen's was like other churches in that it had another door, the secondary one opening onto a porch on the south side. Such doors were usually not barred, and that proved to be the case today. Stephen entered through the south door and drew his horse behind him. He left the door open.

It was a fining offense to bring a horse into a church, but no one was there to object, as was the usual case after the end of the midday service. It was dim in the church, shafts of light streaming down from the narrow side windows, leaving rectangles of yellow sunlight on the dirt floor.

"Well, Squinty," Stephen said, voice echoing in the hush. "It's good to finally meet you."

Squinty spun about, surprised to find him behind her. She had been watching the main door, expecting him to enter that way.

"I'm a busy woman," Squinty said. "I don't have time for your nonsense."

"Yes, I expect you are. Queen of Grope Lane, I've heard you called. That is a lot of responsibility."

Squinty smiled, which rendered her frog-like face even more frog-like, as if she contemplated a fly that she was about to finish off. It was hard to imagine that a handsome boy like Martin had come from her.

"You heard me called that?" Peg asked.

"It's true, isn't it? You run Grope Lane?"

"I do, and many other things besides."

"Like the roofers?"

"They pay me tribute so as not to get into trouble with the authorities. How do you know about them?"

"I had a run in with a pack of them in Ludlow a while back. They were from here."

"Ah, yes. Ollie, that boy who died in Ludlow. I don't let them do jobs in Hereford. Not a good idea to foul the nest, you know."

"And I expect you're also involved in a little robbery yourself."

"I thought you had no interest in that. Though I find that hard to believe, you being a crown officer."

"I'm no longer a crown officer. In fact, I'm in a bit of trouble myself, and am dodging the sheriff. But you already know that."

"Which is why you choose this curious place for a meeting, and why you relied on your legless friend rather than coming yourself. You can't move about the city without being spotted." Peg chuckled. "It's almost like you're one of us now — on the dodge."

"I suppose so. For now."

"So what is it you're up to? Hal said you're after those who killed Martin and his patron."

"That's right. And I thought you'd have an interest in that."

Peg shrugged. "I don't give a fuck about Martin. Hanging around that rich man he got too big for his stockings, boasted that he was destined for greater things than working for the family, like a good son should."

"His refusal to help with the robbery the last straw for you?"

"Yeah. It would have been rich if FitzHerbert had blamed the loss on him." Peg laughed.

"And you had nothing to do with their deaths?"

"I already told your gimp boy Harry that."

"It was the truth?"

"What do I have to do, cross my heart and swear before God?"

"I won't make you go that far. So then, who did?"

"Did what?"

"Who killed FitzHerbert and Martin."

"Don't know. Everyone says FitzHerbert killed himself after murdering that lout of a son of mine."

"You don't believe that, do you?"

Peg was silent for a few moments. She gnawed on her lower lip. "Nah. I don't. Not really."

"I don't believe you don't care what happened to Martin. I know you are concerned about the loss of what he brought in. Don't you want to know what really happened?"

Squinty shrugged. "There probably won't be nothing I can do about it."

"Knowing is better than not."

"I don't have much that will help."

"Maybe you don't. Maybe you do. Was there anything going on in the household? Any disputes between FitzHerbert and anyone else?"

Peg crossed her arms. "Look, if you think Martin kept me up on every little drama of the FitzHerbert household, you are much mistaken. I only saw him from time to time, when he came by to drop off my cut of his earnings. We didn't gossip. You might want to talk to Curthose. If anyone knows the household gossip, it's him."

"Curthose would not be at the honor any longer, I would imagine."

"You are a smart one to figure that out."

"Where can I find him?"

Peg shrugged. "Curthose has a townhouse on Milk Lane near the cathedral close. Third house from the corner. You might find him there."

"And about the letter."

"What letter?"

"You don't know about any secret letter FitzHerbert was carrying?"

"Martin never mentioned no letter."

"No one asked you to steal it for them?"

"We never stole no letter. Are we done now? I'm an old woman, full of aches and pains. I need to get home and get off my poor feet."

Peg stepped toward the main entrance.

"Wait," Stephen said. "There's one other thing."

"What would that be? You're trying my patience." But Peg stopped and turned to face him.

"Where did you get that sleeping draught?"

"The dwale? Why?"

"I'm curious. I understand that dwale is not common."

"Hamblett's. Is that definitely all?"

"Bought it yourself?"

"Of course not. I had one of my girls do it. I am done answering questions."

Peg hobbled toward the entrance with a wave.

Chapter 18

Stephen went back the way he had come. The clouds were low and scudding. A light rain began to fall, driven by a gusting wind that rattled the branches of the trees and stirred the grass by the road. On such a dark day, you wanted nothing more than to huddle by a fire with a blanket across your knees, safe from the wet and drafts.

It was a day that matched his mood: dark and troubled, and increasingly desperate and devoid of hope. He felt as if he was in a house with many doors. He went around to the doors trying the latches. Most wouldn't open. The few that did opened onto dark passages filled with cobwebs, leading nowhere that he could see. He had been certain that Squinty Peg would provide him with the clue he needed to unravel the mystery of the murder, and through that the recovery of the letter. But she had been one of those corridors that led into the dark, into nowhere. If she was telling the truth. And he had the feeling that she was concealing something. He wasn't sure what. But people like Squinty always lied. It was as if it made life more enjoyable, the fooling of people, a way of demonstrating at least to yourself your superiority over the idiots who believed the lies. But perhaps her lie wasn't important. He didn't know. He had no answers.

After an hour or so, he reached the barn at the crossroads. Even the sight of Harry on a bench within the shed, his face purple with bruises but apparently recovered, did not lift his spirits. Harry's stumps were exposed and he was massaging them with one hand; the other hand held a carving knife and a block of wood that Harry had begun to turn into someone's face. Stephen could see the terrible scars where the barber surgeon had sewed up the stumps, mottled and ragged. He thought about his own injury, his wounded foot, and how it was nothing compared to Harry's.

Stephen took a seat on the bench by Harry. "What are you working on?"

"A girl."

"What girl? Not another of the saint?" At one time, Harry had made small money by carving the likeness of a young woman found dead in the yard of Saint Laurence's Church in Ludlow. She had been as beautiful in death as in life, and people of Ludlow had thought her a saint.

"Naw."

"Anybody I know?"

"You might."

"Can I see it?"

"Nothing to see right now. It's pretty raw." Harry slipped the carving under his shirt.

"Doesn't this place have ale?"

"Not any you'll want to drink," Harry said, passing Stephen his cup. "Try not to choke. And don't spill any. It's the best they have. And cost me good money."

Stephen sipped from the cup. He almost spit out the ale; it was sour enough to make the tongue curl and the throat gag. He swallowed with effort.

"Waste of time with Squinty, I see," Harry said.

Stephen nodded. "Least ways, Squinty and I are good friends now."

"Squinty has no friends. She only has interests."

"Hmm. Reminds me of a sheriff I know."

Harry chuckled. "It's about time he turned his coat again. Care to make a wager on how long it is before FitzAllan runs back to the King begging for forgiveness?"

"More likely, he's waiting to see how big the bribe will be to get him back."

"You think that's likely?"

"They need him more than he needs them."

"I never thought about a King needing somebody."

"A King rules only as long as people are willing to obey him. We're looking now at what happens when many people don't."

"You'd think our good King would realize that he needs to be more generous."

"The problem is that he's been generous to a few and that provoked the resentment of the many."

Stephen stood up and gave Harry back the cup. "I'm going to turn in."

"It's not even sundown. Did the ale make you ill?"

"No, it could poison an ox, but I want to get some sleep. I'm going into town tonight."

"After sundown?"

"Precisely. Wake me when you come to bed."

"What are you going to do, jump over the wall?"

"Not quite."

"But why? You'll just get caught. You don't think for a moment that FitzAllan is going to honor that safe conduct you've got, do you?"

"He probably wouldn't. But I've had an idea. It's all I can think to do."

Harry and Joan woke Stephen as twilight faded.

The rain had stopped and the clouds were broken, revealing a crescent moon low on the horizon from time to time. Stephen went behind the barn and changed into his ratty old peasant clothes. He loved moons like that, just a slit and the remainder of the disk visible as a faint circle in the dimming sky, a few stars already twinkling. He wondered if the moon was as flat as the earth.

Gilbert met Stephen at the corner of the barn. He handed Stephen a butt of bread and ham wrapped in a cloth. "I saved supper for you."

"Thanks. I'm starving."

"Harry said you're going into town."

"Yes."

"How are we getting in?"

Stephen smiled, mouth full of ham. "We? You want to come? You'll see."

Stephen groped beneath the surface of the stream for the first stepping stone. Finding it, he set his bad foot upon the top of the stone. The foot found the water refreshing, for it had begun to ache from their walk from the barn. Gingerly, he made the crossing and sat upon the grass on the other side.

"I'm supposed to do that, too?" Gilbert whispered. "Walk on water?"

"I told you, there are stepping stones beneath the surface."

"What if I slip?"

"Then you'll get wet. But you better not, because you'll make so much noise you'll alert the watch."

"If they aren't watching already."

"I've a feeling this is one part of the wall that is not watched. But not if there's a commotion."

"What if it's deep? I could drown."

"Probably so. It's as deep as your head, so be careful."

"Be careful, the man says." Gilbert rose and tested the water with a toe. He fell backward when it found no resistance, but at least did not cry out or roll into the water. He tried again. This time, his probing foot found the first stone. "Good Heavens."

"Come on, hurry."

Hurry was not in Gilbert's nature, however, especially when an awful death lay on either side, accessible by a simple misstep. Gilbert at last threw himself onto the grassy slope of the ditch, although he would have slid down into the water if Stephen had not caught his shoulder.

Stephen clambered to the patch of vines. He pulled up the wicker cover.

"You first," Stephen said.

"No, you, I insist," Gilbert gasped.

"All right, then. Hold the door."

Gilbert grasped the wicker. "It's like the tunnel at Ludlow," he said referring to a certain secret tunnel that gave access to the castle beneath the northwest tower of Ludlow Castle.

"I suppose," Stephen said, squeezing into the tunnel.

It was unlike the Ludlow tunnel in that it was lined with wooden planks and not stone and was not tall enough for a man to stand upright. Instead, you had to crouch. He scuttled into the dark, feeling his way, knocking his head against the ceiling a few times. Gilbert climbed in and settled the wicker doorway behind him.

Stephen shuffled for some distance until he bumped into a ladder.

"Up we go," he murmured.

He climbed the ladder to a trapdoor. He feared that it might be bolted, but it yielded a couple of inches when he pushed up on it. He listened to make sure no one was about. Hearing nothing, he lifted the door, careful that it should not fall with a bang and alert anyone nearby, and climbed out of the hole.

Stephen was in a small shack. It seemed to be filled with gardening tools. He made out hand scythes on the wall, rakes, hoes, a shovel, an ax, and more.

He crawled to the doorway and kept watch while Gilbert labored up the ladder, wheezing with the effort.

"You were not meant for a life of crime," Stephen said when Gilbert joined him at the door.

"I was most certainly not," Gilbert said. "I was meant to spend life before the hearth with my children at my feet and a book on my lap. But that life is impossible around you."

"My father said I was a bad seed," Stephen said, as he rose and entered the garden. "Always causing trouble. I've tried ever since to live down to his expectations."

"You are an example to us all of what not to do."

"Well, there is Harry."

"I am taking Harry into account."

Stephen paused to get his bearings, then struck off across a pasture of knee-high grass. An orchard loomed to the right, bordered by a wicker fence. Ahead one house had its windows thrown open, candles illuminating people drinking inside. The buzz of conversation drifted across the field. He followed the fence to its conclusion at the rear of the lighted house, where there was a vegetable garden and a privy, unseen but detectable by its signature aroma. As if that wasn't enough, he heard voices in the dark ahead. He lay down against the fence as two men stumbled out of a gap between two houses and made for the privy. The one who got there first took advantage of it. The other, unable to wait, urinated in the path.

Stephen waited until the two men had returned through the gap between the houses, and then went through it himself. He thought it was clear, but he bumped into a whore on her knees servicing a man leaning back against the side of a house.

"Watch where you're going, you drunken sod!" the whore snapped. "You almost made me bite it off!"

"Sorry," Stephen muttered.

The alley opened onto Grope Lane. The surprise was that the lighted house was Squinty Peg's.

Meanwhile, the whore's protests had been heard by others. A brawny fellow with the Squinty face held a lantern aloft at the mouth of the alley. The white face of the whore looked surprised, while her customer looked frightened. They both took off running toward the back garden, pursued by the Squinty boy, who shouted, "You bitch! You're not allowed to work here!"

Stephen pulled his hat down about his ears and walked fast toward Olde Street, despite the ache in his bad foot.

He could breathe easier having got around the corner, but there was still the night watch to look out for, since the church bells around the city began to peel, announcing the curfew.

Indeed, a couple of bailiffs were lying in wait across the street to catch a quick and easy fine. They started after Stephen and Gilbert, with a, "Hey, you! Stop!"

Normally, you only needed to provide an excuse and a financial incentive to avoid arrest for breaking curfew, but Stephen was certain he would be recognized. He took off running as fast as his bad foot would allow.

This was unexpected. The guilty usually just gave up and paid, so he was able to get quite a jump on them. Not to be deprived of their fine, however, the bailiffs gave chase. One grasped Gilbert's sleeve, but Gilbert pivoted and knocked him off his feet with a punch. Now, in addition to curfew breaking, they could add assault of a city officer to their list of offenses.

The other bailiff was so astonished at this that he stopped to help his companion to his feet, and by then Stephen and Gilbert had reached the corner of Saint Peter's Church and turned into Butchery Row.

The assaulted bailiffs began clanging their alarm bells and calling the hue and cry. The guildhall was just ahead, and figures could be seen spilling from the front porch.

Stephen and Gilbert ducked behind a rain barrel and a lumber pile at the corner of the hall as the other bailiffs pelted by in search of the cause of the disturbance.

"That was close," Gilbert whispered.

"We're not out of the woods yet," Stephen said.

When it seemed safe, he stood up and went around the other side of the hall to Coken Row. They kept to the shadows on the north side of the street, crossed Wydemarsh Street and went as far as All Saint's Church, where they turned south toward Eigne Street. As they passed the church's entrance, a figure loomed. Given his previous experience in the dark here, Stephen sidestepped and drew his dagger.

"Stay where you are, lads, if you don't want to get hurt," Stephen said to the two hooded figures who emerged from the portico and then withdrew at the sight of the dagger.

"Oh, dear!" Gilbert panted as he circled around the danger. "I cannot catch my breath!" He bent over, hands on knees, panting like a horse that had run a mile flat out. "This is awful."

"Let's hope this is the worst of it."

And it appeared to be, for they reached Milk Lane without hazarding life, limb, or fortune, apart from having to hide from another patrol of the night watch as they doubled back on Behyndferthewall Lane.

Milk Lane ran south from Behyndferthewall Lane to the northeast corner of the cathedral close. Despite its narrowness and seeming insignificance, it was one of the streets in town where the richest people lived. Shops lined the street, with the great houses behind them. The passage to the great houses consisted of gateways through the rank of shops which were barred at night.

Except for a tavern which was emptying out as they had passed at Behyndferthewall, it was quiet and dark, everyone in the houses along the street having gone to bed.

Curthose's house, according to Squinty Peg, was the third from the corner. However, Stephen had not asked which side of the street it was on or how to find it behind the shops.

"How could you overlook such a fundamental detail?" Gilbert asked as they stood in the street looking from one third-from-the-corner house to the other.

"It slipped my mind," Stephen said.

"Do you think Theo might know?"

"He might."

"I'm not looking forward to a journey all the way to Jews Street and back."

"Maybe we don't have to."

Stephen retraced their steps to the tavern, which was in the cellar beneath a glove-maker's shop.

"Wait here," he said to Gilbert.

Stephen descended the steps to the tavern door and went in. No one was there but the proprietor and his wife, who was sweeping the floor while the proprietor was carrying in fresh kegs of drink for the morrow.

"We're closed," the wife said, leaning on her broom.

"I can see that. I didn't come for the drink."

"We've nothing left to eat, if that's what you're after, then," she said. "The boys cleaned us out an hour ago."

"I've not come for that either. I'm looking for the Curthose house."

"This time of night? Go on. And what would the likes of you have to do with Curthose?"

Stephen paused at a loss for what to say. Then inspiration struck. "I heard he might be looking for a new groom. I've experience with horses. I want to be first at the gate in the morning in case there might be others."

"You don't look the sort who'd know which end of a horse to feed."

"I was a mounted sergeant once, before I got captured in Wales last winter on the Prince's campaign, and lost everything."

"Hmmm," allowed the wife, reluctant to help since former soldiers were suspect as thieves and robbers.

"I'm looking for a situation."

"Go ahead, Bets," the proprietor said. "He looks harmless enough. Tell him."

"It's the third from the close on the right."

"I know that," Stephen said. "But you can't see the house for the shops."

The wife chuckled. "Look for the third large gate from the corner, you fool."

The gate was ajar when they found it. Stephen paused at the opening, for no one left a gate like this open during the night. It was the porter's duty to ensure that the bar was in place before going to bed. Something was wrong.

Stephen stepped into the passage that led to the inner courtyard. To the right, a doorway was dimly visible in the dark. It was not clear if this was the porter's lodging, but probably wasn't. Most likely it belonged to the people renting the house and shop on that side of the passage.

Stephen and Gilbert went on to the courtyard. There was a barn to the right, a well in the middle, a stable straight ahead, and the townhouse to the left. The house appeared to be the usual sort: made of timber upon a stone undercroft, three stories tall.

They crossed the courtyard and climbed the stairs to the first-floor entrance. Stephen paused halfway up. He thought he heard voices in the undercroft. It might have been his imagination, though, but there was a light on in the hall above his head indicating that people might still be awake. Perhaps the voices actually came from the hall and the wind had tricked his ears. He knocked on the front door, but no one answered. When no one came, he pounded on the door. Still no one answered. The door yielded a few inches to the pounding — like the gate, it was not barred as it should be.

A dim light showed in the interior of the hall behind the wooden screen separating the entryway from the hall proper.

"Is anyone home?" Stephen called through the doorway.

There was no reply.

Stephen entered the entryway and peered into the hall. A single oil lamp guttered on the high table at the other end. There were pallets on the floor as if the servants either had been in bed or were preparing to retire, with blankets strewn about haphazardly.

But no one was there.

Stephen ran across the hall to the stairway leading to the bedchambers, alarm in his heart without any reason why he should feel that way.

It was dark as pitch up there, and he had to go back for the oil lamp to see his way. The first chamber he came to was vacant, the bed mussed.

There was a naked man inside the second chamber, bound to a chair hand and foot. His head sagged forward so that his face could not be seen.

Stephen knelt before the man and lifted up the head to see the face.

It was Geoffrey Curthose. His face was badly bruised, an eye swollen shut, and his lips were rent by several great cuts. One of them ran from the corner of his mouth to the jaw as if it had been sliced open with a knife. Blood had leaked onto his thighs and the hands clasped in his lap, one hand a fist and the other enclosing it. Several teeth seemed to be missing.

He was dead.

Stephen stood up, trembling. He was as familiar with death as he was with anything. He had made death his trade for more than ten years, since he had run away from the apprenticeship his father had forced him to take with a royal justice. But this death, the mutilations having occurred while Curthose was alive, shocked him more than he could admit even to himself. It left his mind utterly blank. He had no idea what to do.

Gilbert, even though he was as stunned as Stephen, took the oil lamp from his hands and examined the state of the bedchamber. There were two chests and a wardrobe, and the contents of them both, which included parchments and vellums and clothing, had been tossed onto the floor.

"I wonder if they found what they were looking for?" Gilbert mused. "The letter, you think?"

"What else could it have been?" Stephen asked. "I doubt it's here if it ever was."

His attention focused on the two clasped hands. One might think that they were folded in prayer for what Curthose must have known was coming. But the manner of the clench suggested something protective. Out of curiosity more than anything, Stephen worked to unclasp the hands. In the grip of the fist he found a small medallion. He rose and examined it in the light of the oil lamp. It was a polished iron bear with an arrow in its jaws and a needle-like clip for attaching it to one's coat — a livery badge, the sort of thing that it was becoming popular for the followers of barons and the nobility to wear as a sign of their allegiance. A fragment of green wool was impaled on the clip.

"Who do you think it was?" Gilbert asked, on his hands and knees looking under the bed, oblivious to Stephen's find.

Stephen shook his head. "Anyone — the King's men, Montfort's, they both would have an interest." He tried to put out of his mind the thought that Margaret de Thottenham might have been involved, but he could not. She was a hard woman, and there was no telling how far she would go to get what she wanted. But if not her, then certainly there were plenty of others with a sufficient lack of scruples. Had she adopted such a badge? He had seen the like somewhere, but not about her person or that of her followers.

"We should get out of here," Stephen said, turning toward the door and slipping the badge into his pouch.

"That's the best suggestion I've heard from you in weeks."

They reached the landing for the two chambers below when they heard voices in the hall. Something, a suspicion that if asked he could not have articulated, caused Stephen to blow out the oil lamp, for with the voices there were many wavering lights that could only come from torches.

He peeked out the door. A dozen men with torches were moving about the hall setting fire to the tapestries along the walls. The tapestries flamed quickly, belching smoke, the fires racing up toward the wooden ceiling. In moments, the entire hall was burning and filled with choking smoke; even the stairway that Stephen and Gilbert needed to make their escape had begun to burn.

Satisfied with their work, the intruders tossed their torches away and fled out the front door.

Chapter 19

Stephen and Gilbert backed into one of the bedchambers and shut the door. Stephen laid a bedsheet against the bottom of the door, but it wasn't long before smoke started to leak through the crack at the top. He felt the door. It was hot.

He pushed open the shutters of one of the windows and looked out. It was at least twenty feet to the ground, too far for either of them to jump.

"Push the bed as close to the window as you can," he told Gilbert as he smashed a stool by the table and removed a leg from the shards.

Stephen then cut a hole in the blanket near a corner. As Gilbert lifted the corner of the bedstead, he slipped the hole through the leg of the bed. Then he cut another hole in the opposite corner of the blanket and a hole in the corner of the other bedsheet. He slipped the corner of the bedsheet through the hole in the free corner of the blanket and locked it in place with the stool leg, which he turned in the hole in the sheet hoping this would give strength to the connection. Then he threw the sheet and blanket out the window.

"You first," Stephen said.

Gilbert bent out the window. "No, I insist. You can catch me if I slip off."

There wasn't time to argue. The room had so filled with smoke that it was almost impossible to breathe. Flames shone through the cracks in the door and the door itself was sure to catch fire in moments.

Stephen went out the window and slipped down the rope while Gilbert held the top of it just in case the hold on the bed wasn't strong enough to bear Stephen's weight.

"Now you!" Stephen called when he reached the ground.

Gilbert gauged the distance, which looked more frightful when you were at the top, hesitated, then put one leg then the other through the window and, grasping the blanket, descended with too much speed in his haste to be away from the flaming cauldron of a house. The sounds of cloth ripping encouraged him to go faster.

Stephen caught him with a grunt.

"I think you've broken my back," Stephen gasped.

"You look capable of running," Gilbert said.

He took off toward the back wall of the rear garden at a waddling run.

The back wall was about six feet high. Gilbert leaped for the top but couldn't pull himself up. Stephen got under his arse and pushed.

"Oh! Wait! Not so hard!" Gilbert exclaimed as he toppled over to the other side, the thump of his landing loud enough to wake the neighbors who had so far managed to sleep through the conflagration lighting the sky behind them.

"I'm all right!" Gilbert called. "I'm all right! No dogs! I don't see a dog!"

"Good to know," Stephen murmured to himself as he chinned himself on the top of the wall and flipped over into the back garden of the neighboring house.

They had escaped from the fire, but they were not free and away by any means. Shutters banged open at all the great houses they could see, including the one before them, and people leaned out to gawk at the fire, the flames now having reached the roof. There were cries for the fire watch. Alarm bells clanged from every direction.

There was nothing to do but press across the garden to the courtyard, even if they would be seen. Several people spilling out of the townhouse and the shops and houses along the street — Caboches Lane — snatched at Stephen's sleeve, for they thought he and Gilbert might be servants of the house on fire who had escaped, and demanded to know what had happened.

But Stephen pushed ahead and passed through the gate to the lane without answering anyone, with Gilbert so close to his heels that they both nearly tripped on each other.

Stephen relaxed once they reached the lane and headed north some distance. The streets were filled with people, for a house fire was a source of dread. It might easily spread to other houses and burn the entire town.

"We should be safe in this commotion," he said to Gilbert as they came to Behyndthewall Lane. "I doubt anyone will pay us any mind."

"Back to the tunnel?" Gilbert panted.

"I don't see us walking through a gate, do you?"

"I was afraid you'd say that. I think I'll take my chances at the gate in the morning, if it's all the same to you."

The safest place to hide for the remainder of the night was Theo and Sarah's house on Jews Street. But since Gilbert did not know the city well enough to find it in the dark, Stephen had to escort him. While they had worried about discovery and trouble, the streets were in such an uproar about the fire in Milk Lane that even crossing the market at the head of Wydemarsh Street attracted no attention.

This detour took considerable time, not to mention the half hour to overcome Theo's resistance to allowing Gilbert to remain, so it was approaching twilight by the time Stephen slipped down the alley by Squinty Peg's house and made for the shed at the base of the wall.

He was about to enter the shack when he heard voices within it. Stephen dashed off a few paces and lay in the grass while figures emerged from the shack, visible against the lightening sky even though it was overcast. The figures all bore sacks on their backs that gave the silhouettes a hunchbacked appearance. One fellow tripped and fell, the contents of his sack clattering and clashing. The fellow in front kicked the unfortunate man in the shoulder. There was a sharp exchange of curses and accusations. Then the band disappeared in the direction of Squinty Peg's.

Stephen waited a few more minutes to make sure the coast was clear, then entered the shed. He put a foot upon the ladder leading to the tunnel, but he did not go down.

He withdrew his foot after a few moments of thought and went out of the shed.

Stephen kept to the path along the wall to the Bye Street Gate, where he crossed Olde and Bye Streets and entered the dark maw of Jews Street.

In moments he was knocking at Theo's door again.

Theo stuck his head out of the upstairs window. "What the devil! You again? What do you want? Quick, before the neighbors notice."

"I need a favor."

"Favors for you are always too dangerous and unprofitable."

"Just this one. It won't put you in any danger."

"I doubt that."

"Who is it?" Sarah asked, out of sight.

"That damned Attebrook," Theo said to her.

"What does he want?"

"Nothing good."

"What do you want, Sir Stephen?" Sara asked, sticking her head out the window to get a look at the visitor.

"I need Theo to take a message to someone in the castle," Stephen replied.

"Why don't you have Gilbert do it?" Theo asked.

"Because he'll be recognized," Stephen said. "And questions may be asked about what he's doing here."

"A moment." Theo pulled his head back in the house.

Shortly, the door opened. "All right, come in," Theo said.

"I'll do it," Theo said when Stephen entered the front hall. "But this is positively the last time."

"Thanks."

"And you're to hide in the next yard. There's a rubbish pile big enough to conceal a wagon back there. If anybody notices you and raises an outcry, you run for it, as fast as that gimpy foot carries you. Now, this message?"

Stephen curled up behind the rubbish pile, which was as large and evil smelling as he anticipated, trying to get some sleep before sunrise.

He awakened just after dawn to the chirping of birds, the hoo-hoo-hoooo! of doves, and the distant cry of a cock greeting the day. Several crows fluttered down on the top of the rubbish pile and inspected it for potential food. One of the crows found the remains of a shoe, which it tossed in Stephen's direction with a flick of the head. The shoe bounced down the pile and landed a foot from Stephen's face, bringing with it a small avalanche of something foul and rotting. "You missed," he said, sitting up.

He had been so tired that even the stinging rain that began while he was asleep did not wake him. Despite the chill and wet, he welcomed the rain, for it gave an excuse to pull up his hood, which would make it easier to pass through the city during daylight without being noticed. The wind was cold and blustery.

Stephen stood up, scanning for people in the back gardens that were separated by waist-high wattle fences. He saw no one, but caught Theo peering at him out of a back window. Theo motioned for him to be away, then closed the shutters. Stephen envied the fact that Theo had his breakfast handy, for his stomach ached and demanded to be filled. It would have to wait.

He jumped a series of fences to reach the alley he had used previously. As he emerged onto Bye Street, the apothecary a couple of houses to the left was putting down the shutters on his shop, a signal that he was open for business. Stephen almost turned away from the shop, but the memory of something Squinty Peg had said made him pause.

Stephen went to the window. The apothecary had his back to the window, bent over a pestle. Stephen coughed to get the man's attention.

"Are you Hamblett?" Stephen asked.

"No," the apothecary said. "I am Fulco Hellecoc. What do you want with Hamblett?"

"I am after some dwale."

"The stuff that makes you sleep? Hamblett doesn't make it. He hasn't the skill. I am the only man in Hereford who does, apart from a few monks at the hospital. The recipe is quite complicated. Get the proportions wrong — especially of the hemlock, opium and henbane — and you can kill someone. That happened to Hamblett, which is why the bishop forbade him to make it."

"I see. Did one of Squinty Peg's girls buy some dwale from you in the past week or so?"

"Peg? What do you want to know for?" Hellecoc gave his full attention to Stephen now, taking in his common brown shirt and stockings, and worn cloak and hood: the apparel of a common man without means.

"I had but a few ales at a tavern in Grope Lane. It put me to sleep. I'm not in the habit of falling asleep after a few ales. When I woke up, my purse was empty."

Hellecoc smiled with a trace of sympathy. "And you thought one of her girls put dwale in your ale?"

"Yes."

"Not much you can do about that now."

"I don't know. There might be. If it happened."

Hellecoc shrugged. "Well, for what it's worth to you, no. None of her girls has bought dwale from me for quite a long time. I sell dwale mainly to older people who have trouble sleeping. The younger people, they have no need of it, unless they have been injured and need a barber surgeon to cut on them."

"What about others?"

"You are a curious fellow. So many questions."

"Please humor me."

"The only ones recently were a lady from the castle, the sheriff's current mistress, and that new coroner, Mapuleye."

"Last week sometime?"

"Yes, it was. The both of them."

"Odd, that."

"I don't know."

"Do you have a batch handy?"

"Of dwale? Certainly."

"Mind if I smell it?"

The apothecary looked put upon, but he fetched a box from a shelf and put it on the counter.

Stephen flipped up the lid and lowered his nose to the contents. It had that same flowery aroma he had detected in the pitcher of wine found in FitzHerbert's bedchamber.

"Satisfied?" Hellecoc asked, retrieving his box of dwale.

"Yes, thank you."

"Well, then, be off. Don't you have a job? Or are you a layabout who does nothing but make trouble for working people?"

The inn was called the Black Lion. It was the same one where Stephen had seen Lady Margaret only five days ago, a few doors away from the Wye Bridge. Those five days seemed an age. Stephen didn't realize how tired he was until he thought about that passage of time. He wished he could retreat to Ludlow and settle at his favorite table by the fire at the Broken Shield and put this mess behind him. But it was not close to being finished.

The Black Lion wasn't the Shield. Its floors were dirt and pocked with holes that Stephen had seen trip a few of the unwary, unlike the wooden floors of the Shield, which Edith Wistwode kept neat and swept, harrying all for any dirt or mud they tracked in. But the ale was sweet and the onion soup, with cheese melting in it, was tasty. He dunked another bit of bread smothered in butter into the soup and devoured it with relish. As inns went, it wasn't bad.

The door opened admitting a blast of chilly air pregnant with the tinny smell of rain. "Shut that damned door!" shouted a chorus of patrons reflexively. The ritualistic way they shouted this suggested they did so at every entrance.

The fellow who had just entered was already closing the door behind him. He threw off his hood. It was Walter, Lady Margaret's man.

But he wasn't alone.

Walter's companion was clad all in black: cloak, coat with silver buttons, stockings; even his boots were black. His black goatee and moustache were close cropped and gave his narrow face the appearance of white porcelain. Predatory eyes regarded Stephen from across the hall.

The two of them crossed the hall, weaving between tables and benches. Walter did not sit, in deference to his companion, who settled onto the bench on the other side of the table.

Stephen should rise at the companion's approach, since he was far outranked on the social scale by the visitor. But he remained seated and put a hand on his dagger just in case. There was bad blood between them going back to an incident last year when Stephen had killed one of Nigel FitzSimmons' cousins. Stephen's excuse was that it had been self-defense, but that hadn't mattered to FitzSimmons, who wanted Stephen dead as a consequence.

"Well, FitzSimmons," Stephen said, "I suppose I shouldn't be surprised to see you. Did Lady Margaret send for you?" There was a murky world out there that he did not fully understand. He only knew that Lady Margaret and FitzSimmons were spies for the Montfort faction. Lady Margaret was FitzSimmons' subordinate, but what position FitzSimmons occupied and how much power and influence he had was unclear. What was clear was that he was a dangerous man.

Nigel FitzSimmons knitted his fingers together. "She did. And she was wise to do so. This is too important a matter to entrust to busybodies and meddlers."

"Busybody? Ha! A busybody who has bested you twice. What does that make you?"

FitzSimmons scowled and looked toward the fire. "It seems that I am forced by circumstances to be civil with you. I want that letter."

"If we come across it during my inquiries, I may look the other way. It is a death that interests me, not some letter."

FitzSimmons brought his gaze back to Stephen. There was venom and hatred in that gaze. But Stephen met stare for stare. It was rather, Stephen thought with mild amusement, like the game children played to see who would blink first, but the stakes for them were higher and blinking didn't count.

They regarded each other for some time this way, as if FitzSimmons was used to overawing others and hoped the trick would work here. When he sensed it did not seem to have any effect, he said, "Let's get this unpleasant business over with. What have you learned so far? Or have you spent your time lolling in taverns and now need more money for drink and whores?"

"Would you like some ale? Since you are being civil, I should return the favor," Stephen said, ignoring the questions for the moment.

He waved for cups to a servant of the inn and when he had them, he poured for FitzSimmons and Walter. FitzSimmons regarded the cup as if it had been filled with piss. He did not touch it. Walter did not reach for his cup, either. Walter looked over their heads at the wall behind Stephen. A hard man with a homely blunt face, Walter was a soldier who knew when to avoid attracting a superior's unwanted attention.

"If you're not going to drink anything," Stephen said, "at least let Walter have a go. He's the one I need to talk to, not you."

FitzSimmons hesitated, annoyed, but assented with a flap of the hand.

Walter reached for the cup reluctantly.

"And you should at least let him sit down," Stephen said. "He's attracting attention. I thought spies were not supposed to attract attention."

FitzSimmons flapped a hand again. Walter slipped around the table and sat beside Stephen. Sitting beside FitzSimmons could have been taken as far too familiar.

"That's better," Stephen said.

"Let's get this over with," FitzSimmons said. "We haven't a moment to waste."

"All in its due course," Stephen said. He extracted the medallion from his pouch and set it on the table. "Have you seen its like before?"

"What's that got to do with this?" FitzSimmons demanded.

"I took it from Geoffrey Curthose's hand."

"Curthose?" FitzSimmons asked. "His house burned last night. With everyone in it — him and all his servants."

"I know. I was there."

"You didn't have anything to do with that, did you, sir?" Walter, who was as hardened and taciturn as a bull dog, seemed shocked at the possibility that Stephen might be responsible for burning up a houseful of people. But then, how different was that for burning up a church with people in it? That happened with sad regularity in wartime. Walter had been a soldier. He must have seen such things, perhaps had even thrown the brands himself.

"I didn't set the fire. Curthose was already dead by the time I got to him."

"The fire was set?" Walter asked.

"Rub the wax from your ears, Walter. I'm not going to mention it again. Even in a deserted place like this, people can overhear."

"Who did it, then?" FitzSimmons demanded.

Stephen pointed to the medallion. "A gang. I didn't get a good look at any of them. One of them wore this badge. I believe Curthose ripped it from the coat of one of the assailants when they invaded his house."

"And what does this have to do with the letter?" FitzSimmons asked.

"I suspect that Curthose took it. Probably sometime after his master was killed."

"You think Curthose killed him?"

"I can't say with certainty, but I don't believe he did. He wouldn't have engaged me to investigate FitzHerbert's death if he had been involved. But someone else wants the letter as well, and, suspecting that he had it, came for him. He was pretty badly tortured."

"So, someone else has the letter now."

"That sizes things up neatly, FitzSimmons. You are quick."

"Don't make fun of me, Attebrook."

"Just an observation. Now, as to the medallion, I assume you're not familiar with it, eh, FitzSimmons."

FitzSimmons shook his head.

"What about you, Walter?" Stephen asked the soldier.

Walter prodded the medallion with a finger. "Yes, I've seen it before. It's the symbol of Lord Richard de Mychenall. He adopted it recently after his return from Gascony. I understand such badges are popular there."

"Mychenall!" Stephen knew the name, of course. Mychenall was not an earl, but he held enough land in southern Herefordshire and Wales about Cardiff to consider himself one. He had kept aloof from the dispute between the barons led by Montfort and the King's faction. It was a surprise to hear his name mentioned in connection with the letter. What would such a man want with it? "I find that hard to believe."

"I don't know what interest Sir Richard might have in the thing, sir. But there are some in Hereford who owe him fealty."

"Who are they? Do I have to hit you on the head to get it out of you?"

"Very good, sir. The most prominent such person is someone you know — your good friend, Thomas de Mapuleye."

Chapter 20

"Mapuleye," FitzSimmons muttered, his voice thoughtful but concerned. "You're sure?"

"His men wear the badge, my lord," Walter said. "They are all liege men of Sir Richard."

"Why would Mapuleye go to such lengths to get the letter?" FitzSimmons asked. "It does not make sense. He's one of us. You'd think he'd just demand it of Curthose. I'd expect him to tell FitzAllan about it, who would then simply recover it."

"Are there those who would pay to get their hands on it?" Stephen asked.

"Of course," FitzSimmons shot back. "The King's men would pay dearly to know what promises Montfort has made to the Welsh."

"Then the answer is obvious," Stephen said. "He's doing it for the money."

"He must need it badly, if he's willing to commit murder for it, and betray us in the bargain."

"Well, now you know, the thing is in your hands. All you have to do is ask him."

"I'm not sure that things are that simple. If we demand Mapuleye produce the letter, he will deny having it, if he's so bent on the money."

"Perhaps you could offer to buy it."

"And get into a bidding war with whomever he's in contact with on the King's side?"

"It might have to come to that."

"I haven't much on hand for such a negotiation. We cannot depend on FitzAllan to come up with it, either. I'd prefer to get it back by other means, if that's possible."

"Surely, you have other resources."

"We are not the Crown. The King is better provided for in money than we are. We have only the rents from our manors, and that is hardly enough to afford the army that will be needed soon. We must find another way before we stoop to commerce and bribery."

"What about that false money you had made?" Stephen asked, referring to a plot to forge money that FitzSimmons had overseen earlier in the year. "Surely, there must be something left."

"There is some, but it is far away. It will take days, even a week to fetch it here."

"Then I would not waste any time."

FitzSimmons' fingers drummed the table. "Meanwhile, I should have you find the letter for me. If Mapuleye has the letter I want to know. There will be a reward in it for you."

"I will think about that."

"Think hard."

It was still raining when Stephen and Walter stepped onto Bridge Street, the center of which had been churned up to a pasty mud by the passage of many feet and the wheels of carts. He was glad for the rain and not for the mud, which made walking an effort. It was not unknown to stumble into a puddle that looked like nothing but was a deep sucking maw that would yank a boot right off a man's foot. The ground just outside the Black Lion presented a particular hazard, because there was a dip in the road at the doorstep, and a vast pond stretched from one side of the street to the other. Stephen was a canny traveler in towns, however, and knew to keep to the edge of the road where the ground was not as wet or muddy owing to the shelter given by the overhanging upper stories of the houses bordering the street. Walter followed him, lost in his thoughts.

The prudent way to get to his destination would be to pass around Saint Nicholas' Church at the head of Bridge Street to Wrotehale Street, and thence to Wydemarch and around. But Stephen cut across the cathedral close and its graveyard to Castle Street, where the houses of the wealthiest people in the city could be found. This made his journey to Grope Lane all the shorter and faster, a thing to be prized in the cold and wet, not to mention his aching foot, sore from all the abuse it had suffered.

The rain had driven the barkers and street gamblers on Grope Lane to find shelter, but a few of the windows in the brothels were open, since the girls needed a means to call out to passersby for their business.

At one window, a girl draped her naked leg over the windowsill and called out to Stephen, "Hey, handsome! You look so lonely! Come up and take a load off your feet! I'll rub your back for you!"

Stephen blew the girl a kiss. "Another time, sister! I've things to do!"

"What could be more important than a rub down?"

"My duty, I'm afraid."

"Duty — you are such a dull boy."

"What about you?" the whore called to Walter.

"Can I?" Walter asked. "It won't take long."

"No," Stephen said.

Walter grinned and waved to the whore. "I'll be back tomorrow!"

They reached Squinty's house and went in. The hall was like that in any other tavern, inn or brothel, a low rectangular room with a fireplace on the side where a blaze warmed the room, benches near it occupied by persons who should have a job but did not appear to, barrels of ale opposite along the wall, separated by a high narrow table where the drinks were deposited upon order and where they were often consumed.

"What you want, lads?" asked the man behind the bar.

"I'd like to see Squinty. She here?"

"She's here, but she's busy. Too busy for the likes of you, I think."

"I'm more than I appear. Just tell her that Steve would like another word." Stephen put a farthing on the countertop.

The servant pressed his thumb to the sliver of silver, which adhered to his thumb. "You are a generous one," he said with sarcasm. "Don't get your hopes up." But he went up the stairs at the rear of the hall nonetheless.

It wasn't long before Squinty Peg appeared at the top of the stairs and made her laborious, limping way down the steps with much groaning and the assistance of her cane.

Squinty struggled up to him. She regarded him with a squint, which was her usual way of looking at people. She prodded him on the shoulder with her cane. "What you doing here? What do you want?"

"Is there a quiet place we can talk in private?"

"There ain't no privacy around here, not even in the privy."

"You've a cellar. How about that?"

Squinty pursed her lips. "Willie, fetch me a lamp. Master Steve wants to inspect the cellar."

"Is he a rat catcher?" Willie the bartender asked. "We could use one. The place is infested."

"You're something of a rat catcher, aren't you, Steve?" Squinty chuckled.

"I hadn't thought about it like that," Stephen said, "but I suppose I am."

"He coming, too?" Squinty asked about Walter.

"No," Stephen said. "He'll be happy to warm himself with one of your girls while we talk."

"Sir!" Walter exclaimed, surprised.

"Watch that," Stephen said. "I'm Steve here."

"Right. Steve."

"Just be sure to keep your drawers within reach in case we have to leave quickly."

"You've a nerve walking into my place like that," Squinty said when they had settled on barrels in the cellar. It was musty here, and there were indeed the sounds of careful scuttling paws now and then.

"You know, confession does a body good. You should try it."

"What have I got to confess?"

"You told me one of your girls bought the dwale given to FitzHerbert and Martin. But that's not true. Mapuleye bought it himself, and not at Hamblett's."

"I ain't admitting or denying."

"Did he tell you to get the letter when they were knocked out?"

"He never mentioned no letter."

"All he talked about was the money in the box?"

"That's it. He said we could have that."

Stephen drew a clump of linen cloth from his belt pouch. He set the pouch on the upturned barrel between them so that they clinked, letting Peg know there was money in the cloth.

"Did Mapuleye go with you on the job?"

Squinty prodded the makeshift linen pouch. "No, he's too high-toned for that. It was one of his boys."

"The red-haired one?"

"Yes," Squinty said, surprised. "How'd you know?"

"I'm a better rat catcher than I look."

"Could have fooled me."

"What's his name?"

Squinty smiled. "Not that good, though, eh? Hugo. Calls himself Hugo de Norbury, though I don't think he's ever been within miles of the place."

"So, let me see. The girl comes down with the money, and Hugo goes inside."

"That's right."

"And he comes down with the letter?"

"No. He didn't find no letter. It weren't there. At least I heard him say so to the others of his little band as they made off."

"I see. You're a businesswoman. Let's do business." Stephen withdrew another makeshift linen purse from his belt pouch. This one was much fatter than the first one. He put that purse beside the other one. "There is something I need you to do."

Chapter 21

"Will you look at that," Gilbert marveled from his hiding place in the corner of the hall of Squinty Peg's brothel. He prodded Stephen, who was sleeping with his head upon a table.

Stephen lifted his head. Walter had just entered the hall from the street with Hugo de Norbury. They were laughing as if at some joke.

"Look at what?" Stephen asked.

"I didn't think Walter knew how to smile," Gilbert said.

"He doesn't. He's pretending. He's a spy. That's what we spies do. We pretend, and put people at their ease."

"You consider yourself a spy now?"

"I'm trying to. I'm going to need some line of work when this is over."

"At least you're not running away. I was afraid you might do that."

"You'd miss me? I shall cry."

"You're Harry's favorite target. If you run, he'll go back to picking on me. And now that he has a situation of his own, I can't quell his needling with threats of eviction."

"Put Edith on him. She's enough to scare anyone when she gets going."

"I've already tried that. She ignores me, says she has better things to do than to trouble with Harry."

Walter and Hugo talked to the girl who ran the brothel for Squinty, one of her many daughters. The brothel madam presented a selection of girls to them. Hugo indicated one, who curtsied. The brothel manager handed the girl a candle. Hugo took the girl's arm and led her toward the stairway. This brought him close to Stephen, who dropped his head to his arms, just another drunk. Gilbert bent his head as if looking at his lap, but he held his breath, convinced that the charade was a tissue that Hugo would see through at a glance, even though the hall was not well lighted beyond the fire in the fireplace and a few tallow lamps here and there.

Hugo reached and mounted the stairs without giving any indication that he had recognized either of them. Walter, for his part, ruffled the top of Gilbert's bald head as if he were a child and had hair.

"Stop that!" Gilbert hissed.

"Why?" Walter said. "What will you do if I don't?"

"I will … I will …" But Gilbert could not think of anything sufficiently horrid to intimidate Walter.

Walter chuckled and went away with another girl on his arm.

"I will give you a piece of my mind," Gilbert said to himself, "not that it will make a difference."

"If I were you, I'd invite him for dinner and then let Harry have a go at him," Stephen said as he peeked out of the corner of his eye as Walter disappeared through the doorway at the top. He raised his head. "Go fetch FitzSimmons, will you?"

"Right," Gilbert said, rising. "Good idea about Harry and Walter, by the way. Except the part of having Harry for dinner." He hurried out the front door and around to the back of the house to a stairway leading to the cellar, where FitzSimmons and three of his men were waiting.

Stephen climbed the stairs. He paused at the doorway. He had forgotten to arrange the room beforehand. Now he had to guess which one Hugo and Walter had taken. He listened at each doorway. He heard Walter's voice and then another man's at the third door. He hoped that this was the one.

FitzSimmons and his men arrived and crowded close.

"All right, boys, this is it," Stephen said.

He lifted the latch and rushed into the chamber. Both Hugo and Walter still had their clothes on. They were seated side-by-side on stools watching the two girls undress. Walter tackled Hugo and they went to the floor, Hugo shouting, "What the f—" and the girls reeling backward, but remaining silent; they had been told to expect something, but not what exactly, to be quiet and stay out of the way. One of the girls had the presence of mind to snatch up the candle so that there was no chance of setting the house on fire.

The FitzSimmons men piled on Walter and Hugo. The scrum writhed as Hugo struggled against them, but they were too much and soon had him tied hand and foot.

"I'll take the candle, girls," Stephen said. "You can go."

"What is this?" Hugo shouted in the meantime. "I'll have your head for this!"

The FitzSimmons men had him by the arms, although he was still on the floor.

Stephen kicked Hugo in the head. "Shut up until you have permission to speak."

"You mutherfu—" Hugo sputtered, spitting out blood.

Stephen squatted beside Hugo. He tapped Hugo on the nose with his finger. "I saw what you did to Geoffrey Curthose. Pretty clumsy work."

He ran his finger along Hugo' jaw, up to his forehead and around his face to the chin.

There was a message here and Hugo did not fail to get it. His eyes rounded so the whites showed.

"What do you want, pay back?" Hugo said.

"No," Stephen said. "I'm more interested in information."

Hugo' lips worked as if he were formulating a lie, then came together in a thin line. "You were the ones who came in after."

"Yes," Stephen said. "Where were you, by the way? In the undercroft?"

"Yeah."

"Readying the torches?"

Hugo nodded. He spat, "You think that you, a murderer, are going to appeal against me and be believed?"

"I might. If I do, there's a good chance I'll be believed, especially after my case is resolved. Remember, I have the right of trial by battle. I'm pretty good with a sword, and my accuser hasn't the money to hire the best champion. So, the odds are good that I'll prevail. You, meanwhile, have no such right. If I appeal, you'll languish in gaol until the circuit justice gets by. With things in such an upheaval, that could take quite a long time. Years even. It's very common for people to die waiting for trial, don't you know."

Hugo snarled and spat out more blood.

"So again," Stephen asked, "what were you doing at Curthose's?"

"Looking for FitzHerbert's letter."

"Did you find it?"

"No, he didn't have it. He swore that he hadn't taken it."

"You believed him?"

"In the end, yeah." Hugo' voice got plaintive. "Thing was, it wasn't there when I went up."

"Went up — that would be at FitzHerbert's house, the night he died."

"Yeah, but I had nothing to do with that. They were snoring away on the bed when I left, the both of them. Anyway, that girl'd taken the money, most of it, to all account, and the letter wasn't there. That kid Martin told Squinty that it was kept with the money, but it weren't there. Somebody took it."

"Did you search for it?"

"Wasn't time. I heard voices in the next chamber. I thought someone might come out to take a pee. The garderobe was just off the entranceway."

"So, you don't have it and neither does Mapuleye."

"But he wants it bad."

"Why?"

"He says it's worth a lot of money to the right people. And he needs the money. He's drowning in debt. That new house of his in the city cost a pile, and then there's the furnishings. You'd think the King lived there."

"Enough to kill people for it?"

"Well, I don't know. The fire was my idea."

"To cover up the mess," Gilbert said.

"The chamberlain and his wife recognized me, as well. They'd have reported me to the sheriff for sure. Couldn't have that. I'm sick of running. Been running most of my life. This job with Mapuleye, it makes for an easy life most of the time. Are we done now? You got what you need? Can I go?"

Stephen cut Hugo' bonds and stood up. "Sure. Not a peep about what we talked about."

"Right," Hugo said, eyes shifting as he climbed to his feet. He staggered out of the room without a look at any of the others.

"We should have killed him," Nigel FitzSimmons said.

"We might have done, but it would be too easy to connect us with it," Stephen said. He gestured toward Walter, "With him especially. And I can't have that."

"Where does this leave us?" FitzSimmons asked.

"It leaves us with those in the household, my lord," Gilbert said.

"Well, you best get on with it first thing tomorrow," FitzSimmons said.

"There is a complication," Stephen said.

"Well, take care of it and don't waste time."

"I'm wanted myself for a little charge of murder," Stephen said. "I've given surety to appear and answer, but I doubt FitzAllan will honor it. If you've talked to Lady Margaret, you know the story."

"She mentioned something about it."

"I can't move about the city, nor approach FitzHerbert's family, until I have the question of my freedom settled. I'll need your help getting FitzAllan off my back. Does he know your position?"

"No, but he knows I have Lord Simon's ear."

"Then we must see him together right away. Is he at the castle?"

"Yes. He got back from Ross-on-Wye this afternoon."

"Meet me at the castle gate first thing in the morning."

"Very well." FitzSimmons nodded and went out.

"It's a shame to do nothing about Hugo," Gilbert sighed as they shut the door on the chamber and headed toward the stairway. "A man who would burn a house with others in it is certain to kill again."

"I know," Stephen said.

Chapter 22

Stephen got a full night's sleep for a change, and was well rested when he arrived at the castle's main gate a short time after sunrise. The rain had moved on and the sky was remarkably clear and blue, full of the promise of a warm late summer day, awash with sunshine, although it was cold enough at the moment for him to see his breath.

He wrapped his frayed brown cloak around shoulders and loitered some distance from the bridge over the moat. Some of the workers mistook him for a beggar and shot him a hard glance.

Beggars were not allowed outside the gate except after dinner time, when they were given the scraps from the noon meal. Some of the workers going in pointed Stephen out to the gate wardens and one of them came out to ask his business.

"I haven't asked anyone for charity," Stephen said, keeping his head down out of fear he'd be recognized. "I'm just standing here, waiting."

"For what?"

"I've a job. I'm waiting for the man who'll give it to me."

"I don't believe you," the guard said. "Be away or you'll earn a knock on the head."

"Ah, here he is now," Stephen said, relieved to see Nigel FitzSimmons, in black from head to toe as always, striding through the gate.

"There you are," FitzSimmons said as he drew up.

"Sir," the guard asked, "do you have business with this reprobate?"

"I am afraid I have," FitzSimmons said. "Come along!"

"Right, sir!" Stephen said.

It was a long walk across the bailey to the hall. FitzSimmons walked fast, and Stephen had to struggle to keep up.

"Walk behind me," FitzSimmons said, as he noticed others making their way toward the hall from their accommodations in the towers. "It's an embarrassment to be seen with you."

"Is it me, or the way that I appear? No, I'll wager it's both." They reached the stairs to the hall. "Well, we're here. You first, since you insist."

The hall doors were open as doors often were in good weather, and the servants were setting up tables and putting out benches for the breakfast of those privileged enough to dine in the hall. The fire burned high on a pavement of stones before the dais, giving warmth to the cluster of the early arrivals near it.

Stephen threw back his hood as he entered. Someone gasped, heads turned in his direction.

A servant dashed up the stairs as Stephen and FitzSimmons reached the hearth.

"Good Lord, Attebrook," a minor lord holding a manor in the southwest by the Abbey Dore sputtered, "what has become of you!"

There was a great deal of muttering and disapproval from the other minor lords and gentry present, since it was never done to wear the shabby clothing of the lower classes, even if staring poverty in the face. The words "The disgrace ..." and "shameful" could be heard more than once, although there were a few who regarded Stephen thoughtfully and made no comment.

Percival FitzAllan appeared at the top of the stairs. He gazed down at the spectacle with his hands on his hips with a triumphal air. "Surely, Attebrook, you can't have come to give yourself up."

"No," Stephen said. "We have other business."

"Other business?" FitzAllan asked as he descended. "We have no other business."

Stephen handed FitzAllan the copy of the surety he had received from Walter Henle. "First, there is this. I have given surety to your deputy to answer the charges against me, and it has been accepted. A copy of it was sent to Windsor."

"To Windsor," FitzAllan said, bending over the parchment and pretending to read it. "Why should I care about that?"

"So his grace the King will know of your high-handedness with his loyal subjects. Perhaps he will reflect on your fitness for your post."

"You are impertinent."

"The prospect of rotting in your gaol has damaged my manners, as I am sure it would do yours if things were turned about."

"All right, then." FitzAllan's fingers brushed the document away. "That's one trick played. Are we done? Must you ruin breakfast with your presence? Especially as … undressed as you are?"

"There is something more."

"What?"

"I was asked by Geoffrey Curthose to look into the manner of Lord Rogier FitzHerbert's death."

"I think you can put aside that pledge. He's no longer with us. Burned up in his house, I'm told."

"Yes, it was a tragedy. But I made a promise to him that lives on, and there are others who are interested in this inquiry, like Sir Nigel here."

FitzAllan's attention had been so fixed on Stephen that he had not noticed Nigel FitzSimmons standing right behind him.

"Your pardon, Sir Nigel," FitzAllan said. "But what has this person to do with you?"

FitzSimmons cleared his throat as if what he had to say caused him difficulty. "It is not so much what Attebrook has to do with me but with our common cause. Kenilworth is interested in the truth about Sir Rogier's death. There is doubt that he killed himself, and suspicion that someone might have murdered him." The reference to Kenilworth left no one in doubt about whom FitzSimmons spoke: Kenilworth was Simon de Montfort's stronghold and where he made his base.

"Murder? Why, for God's sake?" bellowed FitzAllan.

"That is something Kenilworth dearly wants to know, and why I was sent here. To further that inquiry. I trust you will not interfere."

"I have no interest in interfering with something deemed so important."

"That includes leaving Sir Stephen to do as he must."

"Does it?" FitzAllan stroked a lip. "I suppose. As long as he does not escape justice in the end. He's a dangerous fellow, I must warn you. Trouble follows him around like a bad smell." He chuckled. "As you know to your own loss."

"I understand," FitzSimmons said. "I understand very well."

"Will you keep me informed of how things are going?"

"Certainly."

"Oh, and Attebrook, how did you get out of gaol?"

"I am good at picking locks," Stephen said.

"And at lying, too," FitzAllan said. "Well, I'll have it out of you eventually."

"No, you won't."

Chapter 23

"Just like you two," Harry said as Stephen sponged himself down in the barnyard in preparation for putting on his usual clothes. "You missed the biggest thing to happen around here since King Henry came to visit — lolling around in the town enjoying its fruits rather than carrying on a proper investigation as you were supposed to do, leaving the hard work to me."

"What are you talking about, Harry?" Stephen asked as he wiped his face with a wet rag and then his shoulders. He wished it was warmer. He could no longer see his breath but it was still chilly, even though the day was two hours old now.

Harry waved a hand toward the monastery buildings visible behind a line of columnar poplar trees planted to form a fence around the core structures of the priory, some of the leaves beginning to turn a brilliant yellow-orange at the edges. "There! Go see for yourself!"

"What hard work was that, Harry?" Gilbert asked, gazing in the direction indicated.

"Why, I had to climb on a stump and turn around," Harry said. "And then I had to ride over on the back of my pony over there to get a closer look."

"You managed all that without help?" Stephen asked. "I am impressed."

"Yes, and I didn't fall off. It was quite thrilling, although I risked death to do it."

"What will we see if we go there?" Stephen asked.

"A plot of newly turned earth."

"My, that is suspicious," Gilbert clucked, "especially since it's a bit early for autumn plowing."

"Where is this turned earth?" Stephen asked.

"In the cemetery," Harry said. "All the monks turned out to see off whoever they planted there. It was at night. Who holds a burial at night? All the candles made a great show."

"You know who it was?" Stephen asked, although he could not see what relevance the answer might have.

"I have a good idea, but you may want to ask the prior about it."

"Care to give us a hint?"

"No. I've done enough. I'm tired now. Joan! Are there any of those eggs left?" Joan, who was in the barn, could not be heard to answer. "I guess she can't hear me," Harry said, letting himself down from his stump, and swinging toward the barn on his fists.

"Should we go see?" Gilbert asked.

"I suppose," Stephen said. "It shouldn't take long."

"They buried someone at night, by candlelight," Gilbert mused as they trudged along the narrow cart lane to the priory. "Who would merit such a funeral?"

"I have no idea. Probably one of their own who died of the plague. Who else would they need to plant so quickly? Dead and done, that's what it sounds like."

Gilbert stopped dead. "You think there's plague there?"

"Could be." Stephen grinned. He tugged Gilbert's sleeve. "Come along. We won't be long. We can shout our questions through the door if you're worried about contagion."

"A person with his wits about him always worries about contagion," Gilbert said.

The lane ran through the fence of poplars, which was even more grand and imposing close up, and straight through an actual fence of stone. Stephen pressed into the yard and stopped at the porter's house at the outer gate.

The porter's assistant made them wait while he fetched that august official, who took his time about showing up.

"What can I do for you, sir?" the porter asked, taking Stephen's measure and putting him where he belonged on the social scale, which was the minor gentry.

"Anyone die here recently?" Stephen asked.

"Die here?" the porter asked. "No."

"No cases of the plague?" Gilbert asked anxiously.

"Good Heavens, no! What have you been hearing?"

184

"Nothing about the plague," Stephen said. "But there was a burial here the other night, before the rain. In the dark."

"I don't know about that, sir. I retire early. Soon as the sun goes down, it's bed for me. I've got to be up early, you know. Lots to do. Though I did hear some singing. I thought it was Compline, though it seemed a bit late for that."

"Well, then," Stephen said, "I'd like to talk to the prior."

"I'm sure he's busy, yes, very busy."

"Of course, he's busy. But I'll have to ask him to give me a few moments."

"I suppose it don't hurt to ask if he's free. This way, then."

The priory was like any other, the church, a small stone affair that could be mistaken for a simple dwelling, on the south side, with the range — refectory, dormitory, kitchen, scriptorium, and chapter house — on the north.

A cemetery lay within the outer stone wall to the south of the church, but Stephen did not spot any fresh grave.

They went through into the cloister and crossed on a gravel walk of white stones to the chapter house.

"If you would wait here, sir," the porter said, and went inside.

He emerged after some time and admitted them into the house. The ground floor was the meeting room for the brothers. There couldn't be more than a dozen or so, judging from the few benches there. They climbed a stair at the side to the first floor, where the porter knocked on the door and received permission to enter. He opened the door and shut it when they entered.

The prior, a large bronze cross on a chain around his neck, had turned from the window where he was writing something, a pen still in his hand.

"Careful there," Stephen said, pointing to the pen, which was about to drip ink on the prior's habit.

"Ah!" the prior said, snatching up a rag to catch the drip. "Thank you. Ink stains are such a problem to get out sometimes."

"A hazard of the profession," Stephen said. "But not eradicable without some scrubbing. It's the ink under the fingernails that's really hard to get off."

"You do not look the sort to have been much at risk from such a mishap," the prior said, setting down his dangerous pen. "If I had to judge, you have more the air of a man of war."

"I've been that. Before that I spent a short indenture as a lawyer's clerk."

"And you ran away, I'll wager. Not that I can blame you. The law can be tedious stuff." The prior smiled. "I have no aptitude for it myself, which is why you find me in these modest circumstances and not at the cathedral or some other grand place. Now, what brings you to our house? The porter mentioned you had an interest in our recent burial. Who are you, that this matter should concern you?"

"I am Stephen Attebrook of Ludlow. And I suspect you know my interest."

"I see." The prior folded his hands in his lap, his face troubled. He drummed his fingers on the table while gazing out the window at the brilliant fence of poplars. "What gave it away?" he asked at last. "It is supposed to be a secret."

"I have a confidential informant. You buried him two nights ago, by candlelight, you and I believe all the brothers."

Gilbert tugged at Stephen's sleeve. "Him?"

Stephen smiled, for now he knew why the burial was important. For Gilbert's benefit, he said, "It was Sir Rogier after all. It is in consecrated ground, is it not?"

The prior nodded. "Out there. It is a pleasant spot, by the fence near the poplars. Sir Rogier was the one who had the trees planted when he was a young man. He was fond of them. He told me once of the pleasure he got from seeing them sway in the wind across the field."

"I trust that he endowed the priory with other benefits?"

"He had our church built as well. It is a small thing, but there are not many of us."

"And the hospital, too?"

"Yes, without his generosity, we could not have begun that good work."

"And you allowed his burial in consecrated ground because you know he did not kill himself, not because of his generosity."

"It would have been sinful otherwise. But I believe strongly enough in it to give his lordship a decent resting place. Not some hole in the ground near a rubbish dump, which is what had been planned for him."

"Why do you believe it?"

"I cannot tell you."

"This is not a belief you got out of thin air."

"No, it isn't."

"You were not there that night."

"Of course, not."

"So, you spoke with someone who was."

"I heard a confession from someone who was."

"You are a priest as well?"

"The priesthood is not required of a monk, but I am one, so that the Holy Mass can be said here, and all the rites of the Church performed."

"The name of that person would not violate the confidentiality of a confession."

"I feel it would in this instance."

"You are shielding someone who can help solve his murder and catch his killer."

"That is the price that must sometimes be paid."

"Did you fetch the body yourself?"

"Or any of the brothers?" Gilbert added.

"No," the prior said, looking uncomfortable.

"Your informant brought the body here," Stephen said.

The prior looked even more uncomfortable.

Stephen plowed on, "The act of bringing a body here is not a part of a confession."

The prior sighed. "No, it is not."

"So, you are not bound by considerations of confidentiality as to the name of that person."

"I am bound by considerations of prudence and friendship."

"Friendship ..." Stephen rolled the word around on his tongue and in his mind until its full import struck. "So, Sir Rogier's chaplain brought his coffin here."

The prior looked pained. He nodded. "Father Philo."

"Do you know why Father Philo has not come forward with his testimony?" Stephen asked.

"That I cannot say."

"I do not remember questioning a chaplain," Gilbert said as they made their way back to the Leominster road. "Did you?"

"No, and I suspect he was not in the house when we and Mapuleye arrived. He hid himself because he did not want to be questioned, and to give lies for an answer."

They reached the road and turned toward the city, the north wall and gate a brilliant white even though draped in shadow for most of its length.

It was but a short walk to the lane leading to the FitzHerbert manor house. They entered the yard. Stephen looked around. It was quiet. No one seemed to be about: not in the kitchen, the brewery, the barn or the stable. He heard voices behind the house and realized that all the villains and freeholders were out harvesting apples in the orchard.

He crossed to the little chapel, noting that there was no graveyard about it as was often the case with family chapels. It was a well-built little place with a small tower that was more ornamental than functional; church towers often served as defensive hiding places in time of trouble, the whole whitewashed and clean, nor any moss on the roof shingles as if from time to time some poor servant had to get up there and sweep them off.

"Look at the windows," Gilbert said. "They are paned with colored glass!"

This was indeed an extravagance, but it was growing popular to fill church windows with glass.

"It won't be long before the rich put glass in the windows of their houses," Stephen said, striding toward the side door.

He glanced in. It was deserted.

Gilbert peered around the jamb to get a look too, and he gasped, for the colored glass — reds, greens, blues, yellows — transmuted the raw sunlight in a wondrously colorful way, sending down shafts of multiple colors that mingled on the dirt floor. "Will you look at that!"

"They have the same at the Hereford cathedral, you know. Only the panes are put together to make figures and to tell stories from the Gospels."

"I've heard. I should like to see it."

"When we're done with our work, we'll go there."

"That would be wonderful."

There was a large timber house of one story behind the chapel. The outside was freshly plastered, and the thatch was well-cared for. It had to be the chaplain's house. So, Stephen went there and knocked on the door. He heard shuffling inside and presently the door opened, revealing an old man, hair gray and thin about his ears, a long nose made longer by an emaciated face, the back stooped so that the top of the tonsured head came no higher than Stephen's shoulder.

"What can I do for you, sir?" the old priest asked in a reedy, shaking voice.

"You are Father Philo?" Stephen asked.

"I am. And you are?"

"Stephen Attebrook."

"Ah, I thought so. My eyesight isn't what it used to be. And I suppose you want to talk to me."

"I do."

"Well, you might as well come in. I cannot offer you refreshment, I am afraid. I have used up the last of my ale and in any case, my servant girl has gone out to the apple harvest." Father Philo wagged a finger in the air. "Nothing like the apple harvest! Soon we'll have cider!"

It was a substantial house, large and spacious, divided into a hall and adjoining rooms. There was even a large wooden chair with cushions before the hearth.

Father Philo settled onto one of the benches at the table in the hall, and Stephen and Gilbert took places on the other side of the table.

"You've come to ask me about Sir Rogier," Father Philo said. "I had expected you earlier, but then I heard you'd had a spot of trouble yourself. Has that been resolved?"

"Not completely."

"Well, I am sorry. What would you like to know?" Father Philo smiled. It gave his face a benign, even friendly appearance. "I don't think there's much I can tell you that will help."

"I spoke to Prior Hamelin," Stephen said. "He told me you brought Sir Rogier's body to be buried in the church cemetery two nights ago."

Father Philo's smile disappeared. "Oh. You know about that."

"Prior Hamelin would not have allowed a suicide to be buried in consecrated ground, except he says you swore that the death was not suicide."

"He broke his vows when he said that!"

"I deduced what you said from what little he told me. How do you know Sir Rogier's death was not suicide?"

"I have sinned," he said. "I do not know it wasn't a suicide. Although I don't believe it."

"So you lied to Prior Hamelin," Stephen said.

"Yes. The sin is mine. But I will bear it for the good his father did for me. You know what happens to the souls of those not buried in consecrated ground! They are doomed to wander the earth or sink into Hell! They have no chance for God's redemption. I could not let that happen to his lordship."

"You have served the family a long time?"

"I was a villain of the family. But Lord Serlo, Sir Rogier's father, saw fit to sponsor my education and celebrated my ordination on condition that I remain and be the family chaplain and provide care and comfort for the people living and working in this parish."

"You agreed to this?" Gilbert asked.

"Gladly."

"Were you here the night Sir Rogier died?" Stephen asked.

"I was."

"Is there anything you care to tell me?"

Father Filo shook his head. "I slept soundly that night. I never had to get up once, which is unusual. I rise often during the night. It's an old man's disease, being unable to sleep."

"Did you see or hear anything unusual?"

"As I said, I slept through the whole night."

Stephen went to the window and studied the manor house. "Are Lady Aleusa and Lady Isabel here now?"

"No. They left three days ago."

"Which is what enabled you to move Sir Rogier's body without them knowing."

"You suspect me of too much cunning."

"Where did they go?"

"To her dowry manor. A place called Hawkley. When you see them, you won't say anything about Sir Rogier's resting place, will you? I'd rather Lady Aleusa not know."

"I have no reason to mention it."

"Thank you."

"There is one other thing I've just remembered. Was Albert Ferrand here on the night of Sir Rogier's death?"

"No. Lady Aleusa sent for him afterward. His lordship refused to have him in his house."

"Why?"

"The rumor is that Ferrand is Lady Aleusa's son."

"Her son?" Stephen asked confused. He had been under the impression that Sir Rogier was his father's only male descendent. Then it occurred to him that like his niece, Ida, this Ferrand was the issue of a previous marriage. "She was married before?"

"No. When Lord Serlo was on crusade, she whelped a child by a fellow called Adam de Bebyngtone. Went off to a nunnery to have the bastard, hoping that no one would find out. But her maid told me about it on her deathbed. Had the boy taken on by someone on her father's estate and raised there. When Ferrand was older, she brought him into her service. Sir Rogier found out the truth somehow. He was furious and ordered Ferrand and Lady Aleusa away. She has not visited since."

"So what was Lady Aleusa doing here?"

"His lordship summoned her and Lady Isabel."

"Summoned them?"

"Yes, they have been at Hawkley during Lady Isabel's confinement and delivery."

"Why would he summon them?"

"I don't know. He received a letter from Langley Priory that set him off, agitated him more than I've ever seen him upset. Straightaway, he wrote to Lady Aleusa and Lady Isabel demanding they come to Broadstowe."

"What was in this letter?"

"I don't know."

"You didn't read the manor's correspondence?" Often chaplains served double duty as a lord's chief clerk.

"No, I have gotten out of that work lately. My eyes are not as good as they used to be."

"Does your replacement know what was in the letter?"

"No, he told me about it, but said his lordship kept the letter close."

"And what happened when they arrived?"

"They had a discussion in the chapel. It sounded like a row, for voices were raised."

"Could you tell what was the point of it?"

"No. None of us was allowed near. Curthose prowled the grounds shooing everyone away. It was most unusual. I am tired now. Can you have mercy on an old man and let me be?"

Chapter 24

There was no point in remaining at the manor, since enlightenment could only come from wringing the truth from Lady Aleusa and Lady Isabel. But Stephen's feet took him across the yard to the house and up the steps to the doorway.

"What are you doing?" Gilbert panted as he hurried to catch up. "Have you had a thought?"

"I am out of thoughts for the day," Stephen grumbled.

"I was so certain that this Ferrand person was the culprit who went out the window," Gilbert gasped as he strained to climb the stairs.

"He may yet be," Stephen said. "Who is to say the chaplain was telling the truth."

"I thought he was truthful."

"Yes. That's what made me have doubts."

"You are always full of doubts, except when you're leaping to conclusions."

"Who has leapt to conclusions now?"

"Well, I admit my guilt. But I dare you to say you didn't think of it yourself"

"The shadow of a suspicion did cross my mind once."

"And remains, it seems."

"And remains," Stephen agreed. "Until it is dispelled."

He knocked on the door.

One of the resident chamberlains opened it. His eyebrows rose at the sight of Stephen. "What can I do for you, sir?"

"I'd like to see Sir Rogier's bedchamber, please," Stephen said.

The chamberlain hesitated and then stood back to admit them.

"You know the way, sir," the chamberlain said.

The stairway leading to the chambers in the attached wooden tower had two landings. Stephen had not marked this feature when he was here the first time. Why was he always missing things? Weren't the answers in the little details? If he failed to register them, how was he ever to figure anything out? He paused on the first landing, where there was a doorway.

"What is behind this door?" he asked the chamberlain, who was on Gilbert's heels.

"It is a guest chamber," the chamberlain said.

"Was it occupied on the night Sir Rogier died?"

"The Lady Aleusa had use of it," the chamberlain said.

"I understand that Lady Aleusa and Sir Rogier had fallen out."

"That is my understanding," the chamberlain said cautiously.

"Something about her having a child by a man who was not her husband."

"That was said."

"By whom?"

"Many people like to engage in evil gossip."

"Not you, of course."

"Certainly not."

"So, you don't really know."

"No."

"And you have no idea why Lady Aleusa and Lady Isabel came here and what they and Sir Rogier quarreled about."

"No idea whatsoever."

Stephen opened the door and entered the chamber. There was a fireplace in the exterior wall, a poster bed with the curtains tied back, a chair by the window with a cushion, and a table. The walls were plastered and painted with scenes from the Gospels. It was an impersonal room, without the touch that indicated any single individual spent much time there, although with the shutters open it was sunny, bright and pleasant.

"Where were Albert Ferrand's quarters on the night of Sir Rogier's death?"

"Ferrand was not here."

"So much for that speculation," Gilbert sighed, with some disappointment.

"What did you say?" the chamberlain asked.

"You've just conclusively ruled out my favorite suspect," Gilbert said.

"What are you talking about?"

"It's nothing," Gilbert said. "Just forget I'm here."

"Do you have any idea where Ferrand was on that night?" Stephen asked.

"I assume at Hawkley Manor," the chamberlain said. "He is now the steward there. Seems a bit young for such responsibility. Please don't mention that I said so."

"Nothing to worry about. How old is he?"

"Hardly nineteen, the same age as Lady Isabel."

"Are Ferrand and Lady Isabel fond of each other?" Gilbert asked.

"What makes you think they are?" the chamberlain asked in a tone that indicated he had taken to heart Gilbert's suggestion that he pretend Gilbert wasn't there, and had found only disappointment.

"I saw them together once."

"They are friends," the chamberlain said. "I suppose. They certainly know each other. How could they not?"

"Close friends?" Gilbert asked.

"Are you implying something?"

"Nothing. We are just interested in the facts."

"I do not see what that has to do with Sir Rogier's death."

"Did Lady Isabel visit Hawkley often?" Stephen asked.

"She went there quite a lot," the chamberlain said. "She and Lady Aleusa were fond of each other."

"And did she arrive from there with Lady Aleusa?"

"When?"

"The last time she came here."

There was a long pause. The chamberlain said, "Yes."

"And they came without Ferrand?"

"Yes. He fell from a horse and turned an ankle, quite badly, apparently. He has a hard time getting around."

"But he came here quite soon after Sir Rogier's death," Gilbert said. "In a wagon."

"So what?"

"So nothing," Gilbert said. "And he left in a wagon, too, I suppose."

"His ankle pained him," the chamberlain said.

"Did the ladies go with him?" Stephen asked.

"They are solicitous of Ferrand's welfare," the chamberlain said.

"Hmmm," Stephen muttered.

He left that chamber and climbed to the top landing, where he went into the small entrance hall.

The door to FitzHerbert's chamber had been removed and not replaced. Instead of crossing to that chamber, he entered the other one. Although it faced north and did not get direct sun, it was bright and cheerful. It seemed that everything was yellow, the yellow wood of the carved bedstead, its heavy embroidered curtains, a yellow-painted wardrobe decorated with painted red poppies. Floral scenes were painted on the walls. A yellow porcelain washbowl rested upon a polished wooden stand by the window, which overlooked the yard.

As Stephen advanced into the room, he became aware that there was more than one bed. Behind the door, there was another. This one was plain, without carved decorations or curtains, yet it too was yellow, including the embroidered woolen blanket that covered it. There was a cradle beside it, also with a yellow blanket. Across the room beside the wardrobe was linen pallet and blanket on the floor, the sort of thing used by a servant. The nursemaid's?

"Who sleeps there?" Stephen asked the chamberlain, indicating the bed by the cradle.

"That is Lady Madeline's bed," the chamberlain said.

Stephen stared down at the bed, his mind in turmoil. It was the sort of agitation that preceded some revelation, some idea. Yet nothing floated to the surface, well, not quite.

He strode to Lady Isabel's bed and sat down.

"What are you doing!" cried the chamberlain.

"I am thinking," Stephen replied, although the thoughts that rushed through his mind were fragments that did not amount to anything meaningful. "Gilbert, take the gentleman into FitzHerbert's chamber. And talk."

"Talk," said Gilbert, perplexed.

"Yes, about anything, sing a song. Just so noise comes out of your mouths."

"You have gone daft," Gilbert said. He tugged at the chamberlain's sleeve. "If you wouldn't mind humoring Sir Stephen? He has fits like this from time to time and the only thing to do is not to arouse him with your resistance. Pretend he's being perfectly sensible."

The chamberlain looked as though he was about to summon help to remove Stephen from the bed, but instead, he left with Gilbert.

Stephen shut the door and sat back down on the bed. He could hear voices through the walls. He couldn't make out what they were saying, but he could tell Gilbert's voice from the chamberlain's.

Just so, he thought.

He was about to stand, but he noticed the cord holding the curtains open. There was one such cord for the six curtains securing them in loops of four about each curtain — four curtains on the sides and two at the foot. It was a lot of cord for the task assigned to it. He examined the cords closely. They were yellow, of course, and appeared to be made of dyed linen. They were about as thick as his thumb. He unfastened all the cords and tied them end to end. Then he hung the resulting rope out the window. It just reached the ground. Disappointed, he pulled the cord back in and tossed it on the bed, mindful of the chamberlain's probable reaction.

Stephen went into the master chamber. Gilbert halted in midsentence at his appearance.

"What was that about?" Gilbert asked.

"I'll be more sure in a moment," Stephen said. He examined the cords restraining the curtains on the bed. They were a different cord from the one that had been there before, blue and green, rather than purple and silver. He unfastened them over the chamberlain's protests and tied four of the six together. He tied the resulting rope to the leg of the bed where he and Gilbert had found the damaged elephant carving, and dangled the end out the window. It came to no more than half way to the ground. "Just so," he said aloud. "I hope."

"Just so, what?" Gilbert asked.

"Gilbert, why do you persist in wasting my time with such questions?" Stephen said. "We must get to Hawkley."

Chapter 25

Stephen did not know where Hawkley was. But an inquiry of Prior Hamelin gave him two routes to get there. It lay about six miles north of Hereford off the road to Leominster at the foot of Dinmore Hill, the great eminence that was so steep in spots that carts and wagons struggled to make the summit and then struggled not to run out of control on the way down. But the manor lay across the River Lugg, which ran along the northeastern foot of the hill, and since there was no convenient way across the river at that point, the few people traveling to Hawkley usually took the road through Sutton Saint Nicholas and on to Bodenham.

"Take the road north out of Bodenham and go left at the first fork," Prior Hamelin said. "The road runs straight to Hawkley from there. A blind man couldn't miss it."

The road through Bodenham was longer, though, so Stephen, who could not abide delay, and Gilbert rode toward Leominster and climbed Dinmore Hill, which offered a pretty view on its precipitous southeastern slope of the Lugg valley, the fields blond with stubble and the trees turning yellow, orange and red.

"Will you look at that!" Gilbert exclaimed as his mule plodded upward.

"Look at what?" Stephen muttered.

"The valley!"

"What about the valley?"

"It's quite beautiful."

Stephen glanced over his shoulder at Gilbert, who was turned in the saddle to admire the view. "Just don't fall off. The view isn't worth it."

"One must take risks for beauty," Gilbert said, gripping the pommel for support as the mule shied out of the way of a wagon coming their way at a speed that was not good for the wagon or anyone nearby.

"Huh," Stephen said, too preoccupied with thoughts which left no room for the admiration of nature.

He didn't even remember reaching the summit of the hill and heading down until they passed above a small village on the western slope of the spur the hill extended toward Leominster. Then they were in the flatland by the river.

The fields beyond the spur on this side of the Lugg belonged to the manor of Dinmore. A well-used track led away from the road toward the river three-hundred or so yards away, so it seemed no crime to take it.

The track ended at the river, where there was a cut in the bank. A rope stretched across to the weir on the other side, where a mill could be heard grinding away, and beyond the mill were the gray thatched roofs of a village. It was small, maybe ten or twelve houses.

The miller spotted them on the bank. "You looking to cross?" he called to them.

"That was my intention," Stephen replied.

"It's a bit deep here! Wait a moment and I'll fetch you."

He clambered down the weir to a broad, flat-bottomed boat — a ferry — which he pulled across the stream by means of the rope.

"I wonder how deep it really is," Gilbert murmured as the ferryman/miller made his way toward them, thinking that perhaps they could save their money, now dwindling, by foregoing the ferry. "Although I have no enthusiasm for finding out."

"Over your head, probably," Stephen said.

"But isn't the question whether it is over my faithful mule's?"

"You have a way of cutting to the heart of a problem."

"Which is why you need me, now more than ever, when you are so confused."

"I would not say I am confused. Just perplexed. I think I have all the parts, but I cannot work out how they all fit together and what they mean."

The boat was big enough to fit both them and their animals. But when the mule realized they wanted her to set foot in the boat, she refused with all the stubbornness a mule could muster.

Stephen finally uncinched the saddle which he tossed on the boat, and, handing Gilbert the mule's reins, instructed the ferryman to draw away from the shore. Stephen then pushed the mule from behind, praying to God that she would not kick. He had seen people killed from the kick of a horse, and he had no doubt that a mule's animosity could be as deadly.

After much resistance, fore feet dug obstinately into the mud of the bank, the mule at last yielded to persuasion, gingerly entered the river, found that it was not so terrible after all, and swam across with the ferry in the lead, leaving Stephen to admire his cleverness with mules from the west bank.

The ferryman returned to fetch him, happy at the fee he got for making two crossings instead of one.

"If you don't mind my asking, sir," the ferryman asked as he counted his farthings, "what brings you here? We don't often get visitors of your sort this way."

"I am visiting Lady Aleusa," Stephen said. "I trust she's here?"

"Just came back from Hereford the other day," the ferryman said.

"And Lady Isabel and Lady Madeline are here as well?"

"Yes, sir. Shame about his lordship, but Lady Isabel will make a fine new match that's more suited to her now. A great lady she is despite her age, and Lady Aleusa is too, no matter what anyone says."

"Does Lady Isabel spend a great deal of time here?"

"She does, except during her delivery. She was up at Langley Priory then. With Lady Madeline."

"Ah, of course, the maid."

The ferryman put a finger to his lips. "Well, Lady Madeline had her delivery, too."

"What?"

"You didn't know?"

"I am not close to the family."

"She fell pregnant about the same time as Lady Isabel. That's what prompted her and Master Ferrand to marry, so's the child wouldn't be a bastard. Although the marriage is supposed to be a secret. Ferrand's parents are said to object to the match. She died, though."

"She?"

"The child. A stillborn daughter."

"That is too bad."

"It was. There were sad faces around here for weeks afterward." The ferryman beamed. "His young lordship is doing fine, though. Never seen a lad so young with so much hair — and red as a carrot! Not that his lordship cared about the boy. He hadn't seen him until last week, when he summoned the lot to Hereford."

"You'd think he'd come here first thing," Gilbert said. "His heir, after all."

"You'd think," the ferryman said, "but you'd be wrong. But then, the high-born aren't like us common folk. They often don't seem much attached to their children. Your pardon, though, sir."

"My parents didn't care much for me," Stephen said, "so there's nothing to pardon."

"Well," the ferryman said, touching his forelock, "got to get back to work. The grain don't grind itself, you know."

"Don't you have helpers?" Gilbert said, seeing movement inside the mill.

"Course I do," the ferryman/miller said. "But they'll make a mess of things if I don't keep an eye on them."

"Well, those were parts we didn't have," Gilbert said as they led their mounts along the road toward the manor house. "I wonder what they mean?"

Stephen nodded. "I am beginning to have an inkling."

"Do you care to share your thoughts?"

"And be attacked for leaping to conclusions? No."

"Well, have you at least worked out how you plan to proceed?"

"More or less."

Gilbert regarded Stephen with skepticism. "I would believe the less part rather than the more."

Meanwhile, the manor house had come into view a few hundred yards ahead. It was a pretty thing in the flat lands on this side of the river, a timber hall adjoining a square defensive tower, a common plan in these parts which were occasionally visited by the Welsh. Stephen, in fact, had grown up in such a house further to the west where the danger was greater. The hall was surrounded by the usual outbuildings: kitchen, dovecote, forge, barns, stable, sheepfold. The occupants of the sheepfold were visible in the fields beyond the house, the whole picture framed by the rising wooded slopes of Dinmore Hill looming on the other side of the river.

As they neared the house, Gilbert said, "I don't like the looks of that."

That was the fact there were four young men mounted on horses and riding at a quintain.

"We could be walking into trouble," Gilbert said.

"So we could."

"No one knows we've come here. If anything happens to us, no one will know where to look."

"Prior Hamelin would suspect. It would be too late by then."

"Assuming the worst."

"You always assume the worst."

"Well, you're never disappointed that way, and are often pleasantly surprised."

Stephen dismounted and unbuckled the leather bag he carried behind the saddle. It held his gambeson, flat-topped helmet, mail and blue surcoat. With Gilbert's inexpert help, he put on his war gear, throwing back the coif and tucking the arming cap in his belt. He wished he had brought his shield, but, in truth, he hadn't been expecting a fight.

"Do you mind if I wait here?" Gilbert asked anxiously.

"Suit yourself." Stephen mounted and walked the horse toward the manor house.

Gilbert fidgeted and then, unwilling to be left behind after all despite his better judgment, climbed aboard the mule, which bucked as Gilbert settled into the saddle. Stephen turned back and caught the mule's bridle to still him so that Gilbert could settle into the saddle.

"You need a new mule," Stephen said.

"What I need is a nice docile horse," Gilbert said.

"Buy one, then."

"Edith won't allow me to spend the money. She thinks it's a frivolous expense."

"She might be right. She usually is when it comes to money."

"Not with all the traveling you've forced upon me. Dear God, I hate travel. It makes one so uncomfortable — sleeping in barns, dealing with all the rain, the bad food, the prospect of death behind every bush."

"I'll put in a good word for you about the horse. But remember, if you hadn't spent the money on that book, you wouldn't need Edith's permission."

"Do speak to her. I'm sure it will make all the difference."

The land was open and relatively flat so that the men in the manor's yard spotted them long before they arrived. The four men at the quintain stopped what they were doing, fetched swords and were waiting in the yard when Stephen and Gilbert rode through the gate. They regarded Gilbert, a stout little bald man on a cranky mule, with contempt, but Stephen with some caution. Stephen's gear was of the best quality, and marked him out as a man to be reckoned with, even if his companion was much less so.

They were all lean and hard, and had the look of hired men, mounted sergeants and not landed knights. It made sense, Stephen supposed, for a woman living alone to have fighting men about for protection.

"You looking for trouble?" one of them asked Stephen.

"Not unless you care to offer any," Stephen said. "I'm looking for Alfred Ferrand. Is he here?"

The one who had questioned him, jerked a thumb toward the house. "In there. He expecting you?"

"No."

Stephen dismounted, tucked his helmet under his left arm, and strode toward the house.

Gilbert plopped off the mule, and grasped Stephen's reins, which he held out to the fighting men. "Would you be so kind as to take care of our mounts? Thanks so much."

The man who had questioned them accepted the reins before he realized what he had done. He spat in the dirt, threw down the reins and shouted for a groom.

The four men followed Stephen and Gilbert into the hall.

It was deserted except for a muscular, handsome man with auburn hair and a prow of a chin, the same as Gilbert had described seeing in the yard at Broadstowe, seated by the hearth with his bandaged foot on a stool.

"Don't bother to get up," Stephen said, settling onto a bench on the other side of the hearth. Gilbert stood behind Stephen, keeping an eye on the four sergeants.

"You're Ferrand, I take it?" Stephen asked.

"Who the devil are you?" Ferrand asked.

"My name is Stephen Attebrook."

At the mention of Stephen's name, Ferrand's mouth fell open. "Isabel! Madeline!" he shouted. "Come quickly! That fellow Attebrook's here!" In a more normal tone, Ferrand said, "You're supposed to be under arrest."

"I'm on bail. I think we might want Lady Aleusa here as well."

"Oh, she'll come at the mention of your name."

"How are you doing, by the way?"

Ferrand was surprised by this question, since he had not expected small talk. "I'll be on my feet in a few days. It's nothing serious. A sprain."

"Ah. How did that happen?"

Ferrand waved toward the four sergeants. "I was working with that lot breaking a horse. One of them thought it would be funny to pitch a stone at her. She bolted and threw me. I landed wrong."

This raised a chuckle from the sergeants. "Come on, Bert," one of them said. "You've got to admit, it was funny."

"I'll get you back, you bastards," Ferrand said, shaking a finger at them. But there was no actual malice in the threat. It was the sort of thing friends said to each other, rough friends accustomed to hard give and take.

Presently, the women appeared through the door leading to the pantry. Lady Aleusa emerged first, followed by Isabel and then Madeline. Madeline handed a linen rag to a servant girl at the doorway who was holding a baby. They all sat by Ferrand, hands demurely in their laps. Madeline and Isabel avoided Stephen's eyes. But Lady Aleusa held his gaze. She was much younger than he expected. For some reason, he had conjured up a picture in his mind of a woman approaching fifty, even sixty, her jaw square, mouth severe, face lines with the cares of age, craggy, eyes glinty and quick to judge and to find one not measuring up.

But what he saw was a woman perhaps no more than ten years older than himself, face heart-shaped with a pointed chin, dimples on either side of a mouth that looked quick to smile, the small nose and green eyes with light brown brows that regarded him with indifference, as if there was nothing he could say that would harm her. He could see nothing of her hair, which was tucked under a wimple so white it might blind one to look at it in full sunlight, her gown sky blue and embroidered with pearl stars. Yet, there was nothing demure about her expression or her posture. She appeared more formidable than most men.

"I knew your mother," Lady Aleusa said. "She told me once how much of a disappointment you were to your father."

"She never mentioned you," Stephen said.

"I would add that she did not find you a disappointment. She hoped only the best for you. I don't think she would be unhappy at how you turned out. A pity she didn't live to see it." Aleusa smiled slightly. "Well, then. I suppose you are here about my stepson, Rogier."

"Yes."

"What have you found out?"

"That he did not kill himself. Or the boy."

"You're certain of this? How so? Who is the culprit? The wind?"

"I think you know."

Isabel started to say something, but Lady Aleusa snapped, "Be silent! Only I will speak."

The servant girl with the child turned to leave.

"You!" Stephen snapped at her. "Stay."

"You do not give orders here," Lady Aleusa said.

"But I will," Stephen said, "and I will be obeyed."

He crossed to the girl before she could duck out, grasped her arm, and forced her to a bench on his right.

Lady Aleusa shot daggers at the four sergeants and made a brief wave of her hand toward Stephen that all but shouted "do something about this."

Stephen tilted his sword forward with his left hand, a move characteristic of the preparation for the draw.

"Unless you answer my questions, there will be trouble," Stephen said. "In such a confined space, there is no telling who will be hurt."

Lady Aleusa's mouth compressed to a thin line.

The sergeants did not move. They shifted uneasily.

For his part, Gilbert's knees began to shake at the prospect of violence, but he sucked in his breath and made himself look as formidable as possible, which wasn't very.

"This is Sir Rogier's child?" Stephen asked.

"That is Gerald," Lady Aleusa said.

The baby indeed had a full head of hair, but it was more brown, yet with a tinge of red. Stephen had seen hair that color before in this household. He glanced at Madeline.

"When did FitzHerbert learn that Gerald is not his son?" Stephen asked. "Was it the letter from the priory?"

"What makes you think he is not?" Lady Aleusa asked.

"Both Lady Isabel and Lady Madeline were at Langley Priory at the same time, and delivered their babies close together," Stephen said. "But one of them was still born."

"That is true," Lady Aleusa said carefully. "It was a sad time for Alfred and Madeline."

"But Lady Madeline's baby did not die. It was your child, wasn't it, Lady Isabel," Stephen said.

Isabel's hands clutched together, her lips tightened and her eyes closed. But she did not nod nor speak.

"And the prior wrote to Sir Rogier," Stephen went on, "expressing his condolences at that baby's death. A poor little girl."

"This is nonsense," Lady Aleusa said.

Stephen took the linen rag from the servant girl's shoulder. He held it to his nose, then passed it over his shoulder to Gilbert. "Does it not smell of mother's milk?"

Gilbert, sniffing the rag, nodded. "It does."

"What of it?" Lady Isabel asked.

"It is not unknown for women of our class to breast feed their infants, although many women rely on nursemaids for that," Stephen said. "But is not done for a woman of our class to breast feed another's child."

"How fanciful," Lady Aleusa said. "What makes you think that is happening here?"

"Women who breast feed sometimes have … accidents, leakage, that shows on their clothing," Stephen said delicately. "I noted the product of such an accident on Lady Madeline's gown the first day I was at Broadstowe. Then, later, upon inspecting Lady Isabel's bedchamber, I found that Madeline slept there beside Gerald's cradle. That made sense. Madeline would want to be near the child when it woke during the night, hungry, perhaps crying and disturbing the house." He directed his gaze at Madeline. "So, Gerald is your son, isn't he, Madeline, which you and Alfred have passed off as

FitzHerbert's." He paused. "Or rather, I should say that Lady Aleusa determined to pass off."

"We are close family," Lady Aleusa said. "Lady Madeline kindly offered to nurse Gerald upon the death of her own child. She had the milk to spare."

Stephen stood behind the girl cradling the baby. He rested a hand on her shoulder. He felt her trembling. It occurred to him that she knew the truth of things as well as anyone here. But he wanted to have it out of the others.

"I suppose that lie might convince a casual inquirer," Stephen said, "but it is not convincing to me. You see, I have struggled to find a reason for Sir Rogier's death. There is always a reason for murder, even if it is not a compelling enough one for the rest of us. At first, I thought it was to obtain Montfort's letter. Then it seemed to be a robbery plot to obtain his traveling money. But neither of those explanations hold any water. Now, I find I am left with but one explanation. And it is one that is compelling. You pressed Sir Rogier to marry in order to produce an heir for the FitzHerbert family. He struggled to do so, given his proclivity, yet managed in the end. Meanwhile, you had brought your own son, Alfred, into your house, where he fell into close association with both Isabel and Madeline, and due to that association, Madeline fell pregnant. It was simple luck that this happened around the same time for each of them. They even delivered about the same time, more luck still. When Isabel's baby was still born, you hatched the idea to substitute Madeline's boy, a male heir, for the dead child — a male heir who is a grandson of your blood."

Lady Aleusa listened without moving.

"But Sir Rogier found out — oh, that bothersome prior," Stephen said. "Was he fishing for a bequest, do you think? In any case, Sir Rogier summoned you all to explain yourselves. From the sound of things, he was not satisfied with the explanation. Did he threaten to put you out for complicity in this scheme, Isabel, and to denounce the child as not his own?"

"You've spoken to the prior?" Lady Aleusa said.

Stephen shrugged and said nothing.

"So," Stephen said, "we have motive. Yet, there is also opportunity. The baby woke Madeline during the night. She heard voices through the wall, and then there were none when perhaps there should have been. She knew there had been a stranger visiting, who was now gone. Curious, she gets up and peeks in Sir Rogier's bedchamber. She sees Martin and Sir Rogier in a drugged sleep. She tries to rouse them. And then, inspiration strikes. Here is the perfect opportunity to secure all your fortunes. She wakes Isabel and between them, they strangle Martin and then, using curtain cord, they hang Sir Rogier. Even the two of them, being slight women and Sir Rogier so large, they could not hang him high. But it was enough. They then fashioned a rope using the curtain cord from Isabel's bedchamber and the remainder of the cord from Sir Rogier's curtains for Madeline to slip out of the window, using a horse knot to enable her to pull the cord free after she had bolted the door."

The hall was deathly silent, except for the whisper of the wind through the open windows that stirred the women's veils. That silence seemed to last a long time.

"If you bring this charge," Lady Aleusa said at last, "we shall all swear to Gerald's paternity. The prior was not in the labor room, no man was. So his testimony is of no account, only rumor. I shall confess that Rogier's death was my doing, and my doing alone. I awoke to find Rogier in the midst of a licentious union. His proclivity was well known, but I could stand the shame no longer, especially for what it might mean for his newborn son. A stain on the family that could not be washed off in any other way. So, do your worst. I am not afraid."

"No, I don't think you are."

"You aren't going to let him do this, are you?" Ferrand shouted.

"This is the better way, Bertie," Lady Aleusa said. "Say nothing more." Her voice snapped with such an air of command that Ferrand flinched.

"There is the matter of the letter," Stephen said.

"The prior's letter?" Lady Aleusa asked.

"No, Montfort's. You have it. I want it."

"You are clever. It is an incendiary thing, that letter. Have you any idea of its contents?"

"No. Just that it's important."

"Men would kill for that letter."

"They already have. In the name of the King, I demand you hand it over."

Lady Aleusa sat in thought for some time. "Will you tell Prince Edward that we preserved the letter for him? We intended to bring it to him when Alfred was well enough to travel."

"I will tell him you willingly handed it over to me."

"And what about Rogier's death? What will you say?"

Stephen had been thinking hard about this. If he made a presentment against any of them, the likelihood of obtaining a conviction was slight.

"I will be silent on one condition," Stephen said.

"It is?"

"Sir Rogier is now buried in consecrated ground. You will do nothing to disturb that. And you will donate sixty pounds in his name to the priory hospital where he lies." Sixty pounds — the value of two or three manors — was small justice for Sir Rogier, but it would provide a great deal of help to the sick of the parish.

Lady Aleusa's nostrils flared as she considered this. Then she inclined her formidable head. "That is two conditions, but I agree. Madeline, go fetch the letter for Sir Stephen."

Chapter 26

"You don't really believe it was Lady Aleusa's doing, do you?" Gilbert asked as they rode as hastily as the mule would allow on the road eastward to Bodenham. Stephen had not trusted to the ferry in case Ferrand's four friends decided to take action despite what had passed between him and Lady Aleusa.

"No," Stephen said. "The murders were Isabel's and Madeline's doing, probably Madeline's most of all."

"But we'll never prove that."

"No, we won't. The best we can get is Lady Aleusa's confession, false as it is. It will have to be enough, I'm afraid."

Gilbert shook his head. "Aleusa was willing to die so that her grandson can inherit a title to which he is not entitled."

"And to protect Madeline and Isabel. I would not have thought her capable of it."

"Why didn't Hugo find the letter when he ran up to FitzHerbert's chamber?"

"I imagine that Madeline went straight to the strong box for the prior's letter. She found two, and in the dark could not tell them apart. While she was there, she heard Hugo coming up the back stairs and hid behind the wardrobe, or some such thing. Then after Hugo left, they carried out their plan."

Gilbert shuddered. "The cold-bloodedness of it makes me chill. So, what does the letter say?"

Stephen unrolled it on the pommel of his saddle, casting a look behind in case of pursuit. Seeing no pursuit, he read the letter. It was in Latin, but his legal education, brief as it was, afforded him enough Latin to work out the gist. He had read it once, but read it again now. Even on second reading the contents was shocking.

"Come on," Gilbert urged. "Let me see it."

Stephen passed it over.

"Good God!" Gilbert gasped. "I can't believe it! It's … it's treasonous!"

"It certainly smacks of it," Stephen said. "Or could be seen to be."

For the letter proposed to offer a series of border fortresses and lands currently in English possession from Owestry in the north to Skenfrith and Ewyas Lacy and beyond in the south to the Welsh in exchange for troops to swell Montfort's army.

"This will not sit well with the Marcher lords when it becomes known," Gilbert said.

"No. It may be enough to make them switch sides and join with the King."

"What are we going to do?"

"I don't see that we have any choice. We must take it straight to Windsor."

"You're sure?"

"I am a sworn man, like or not, regardless of the goodness of the cause."

"What about Lady Margaret? What about FitzSimmons? What about FitzAllan?"

"I did not promise them anything. I merely promised to look, not to turn over what I found."

"That is a lawyer's hair-splitting. I doubt they will see things that way."

"I suppose not. But that is what I will do."

"Oh dear. Windsor's almost as far as London." Gilbert rose in the saddle to ease a hind end already fatigued. "And you know the way from here so we won't be taking any wrong turns or getting lost?"

"I know the way."

Stephen urged the mare into a canter, and for once, the mule took up the same gait without an argument.

It was indeed a long way to Windsor. And they could not lose any time in getting there.

Epilogue

The letter had the effect Stephen anticipated. When Prince Edward published the contents, Marcher lords by the dozens abandoned the reform party and rejoined the King. These defections gave the King hope at a time when his cause seemed lost. Among those going back was Percival FitzAllan.

As a reward for bringing this letter to the Crown, Stephen received a pardon for what he had done concerning a certain Portuguese ship and any deaths that occurred during the event, including that of William Attebrook. The Prince did not settle the problem of Ida's purported adoption, however. So, ownership of Hafton Manor remained in doubt.

Gilbert, meanwhile, received a purse that went a long way to relieving the money problems at the inn. Edith Wistwode, who did not find out about the illicit book, was grateful for at least a week.

Harry and Joan returned to Ludlow, where Harry resumed his woodcarving business. It was a struggle, but slowly getting better. They were often seen together at the Dinham mill on Sundays after Mass with many other townspeople who liked to enjoy a pleasant autumn afternoon on the green there by the water, and were the subject of considerable gossip.

Matilda and her friends were released from the castle gaol and disappeared, their fellow troupers having long since taken to the highway and left them behind.

Hugo de Norbury was never brought to justice for Geoffrey Curthose's murder or the burning of his house with the entire staff in it. But one night in early October on Grope Lane, someone slipped a knife between his ribs. The killer was never found.

Despite Stephen's pardon, neither Ida nor Mistress Bartelot returned to Ludlow. Stephen wrote to FitzAllan demanding they be freed. He received a reply thanking him for his concern, but that they preferred remaining as guests at Clun Castle.

At Hereford, the Black Friars' Priory received a surprise bequest in Rogier FitzHerbert's name of sixty pounds to be used at the hospital. The monks were stunned to get it, and put the money to work by constructing a new building for the hospital and a dormitory for families of the patients.

Grass grew over FitzHerbert's grave and there was no marker upon it. But the following spring, someone planted an oak sapling upon the grave. It thrived and grew mighty in the years to come.

IF YOU LIKED *MURDER AT BROADSTOWE MANOR,* CHECK OUT THE OTHER BOOKS IN THE STEPHEN ATTEBROOK MYSTERY SERIES

THE WAYWARD APPRENTICE

Stephen Attebrook, a crippled knight facing poverty and ruin, seems condemned to a quiet life when he takes a position as deputy coroner in the small town of Ludlow.

But instead, he plunges into a web of murder and intrigue. A death Attebrook rules an accidental drowning turns out to be a murder, and he must find the killer with little evidence pointing the way.

Then a commission to return a runaway apprentice pitches him into the midst of a conflict between a rebellious earl and King Henry III that is about to erupt into civil war.

Caught up in the twilight struggle among spies readying for war, Attebrook races to defend the apprentice against a charge of murder while dodging killers in the employ of one of the factions.

Thirteenth century England has never been brought more vividly to life than in the pages of *The Wayward Apprentice.*

Available at Amazon at
https://www.amazon.com/dp/B003PPDB12

BAYNARD'S LIST

A secret list identifying the supporters of both King Henry and his rival for power Simon de Montfort has disappeared following the murder of the King's master spy in the west of England.

Stephen Attebrook, the part-time deputy coroner for medieval Ludlow, must find Baynard's list for his former master, the grasping and ambitious crown justice Ademar de Valence — projecting Attebrook into a cesspit of medieval murder, espionage, intrigue and betrayal.

Attebrook faces his greatest challenge as a discoverer of secrets as he races to obtain the list before a rival gets it first, while the life of someone close to him hangs on the outcome.

Available at Amazon at
https://www.amazon.com/dp/B005H86SJW

A DREADFUL PENANCE

War with the savage Welsh is coming to the March, the wild borderland between medieval England and Wales. The English are uncertain, however, where and when the blow will fall. So, Sir Geoffrey Randall, coroner of Herefordshire, dispatches his deputy, the impoverished knight Stephen Attebrook, to the border town of Clun to spy out the Welsh plan for invasion.

At the same time, Randall directs Attebrook to investigate the murder of a monk found dead in his bed at the Augustine priory of St. George at Clun.

The assignment thrusts Attebrook into a tempest of espionage, murder and a desperate feud between the priory and the lord of Clun, while a forbidden love leads to suffering and death.

Available at Amazon at
https://www.amazon.com/dp/B007O9YK2E

THE GIRL IN THE ICE

A sudden thaw on Christmas Day reveals to Harry the beggar a dead girl of extraordinary beauty frozen beneath the snow off the pathway to Saint Laurence's church in medieval Ludlow.

It looks like murder, and deputy coroner Stephen Attebrook, a poverty-stricken knight, feels compelled to find those responsible.

It is a task that propels him into the domain of his worst enemy, Earl Percival FitzAllan, where he must play an involuntary role in the shadow war of espionage and raid being waged between the supporters of King Henry III and the rebellious barons under Simon de Montfort — a game that could cost him his life.

Available at Amazon at
https://www.amazon.com/dp/B00FQ3YXM2

SAINT MILBURGA'S BONES

Stephen Attebrook, the deputy coroner of medieval Ludlow, wants more than anything to be part of an army gathering for an invasion of Wales, hoping for a stroke of luck that will bring him to the attention of some magnate and free him from poverty.

But as the army is about to depart, a castle guard is found murdered at the foot of the castle walls and the precious relic of a saint intended as a gift for Prince Edward goes missing from a locked and guarded chamber.

Stephen's superior, Sir Geoffrey Randall, is quick to volunteer his services to Edward to find the relic. The commission pitches Stephen into the path of a bitter and powerful enemy, Earl Percival FitzAllen. And the search for the relic — and the guard's killer — leads to adventure deep into Wales itself, where Stephen finds the battle he craves.

Available at Amazon at
https://www.amazon.com/dp/B0123KVVD4

BAD MONEY

Medieval Ludlow's deputy coroner, Stephen Attebrook would like nothing better than to enjoy a temperate spring, the Broken Shield Inn's sweet ale and delicious mutton stew. But a murdered man in possession of stolen stamps for minting money is found floating in the inn's privy. And counterfeit money turns up in the hands of innkeepers Gilbert and Edith Wistwode.

Possessing counterfeit money is a hanging offense, and to save his friends from the gallows, Stephen pursues those behind a desperate plot to mint false money — intrigue that stretches into the upper reaches of English society and threatens the throne of King Henry III.

Available at Amazon at
https://www.amazon.com/dp/B01HBZVNJI

THE BEAR WAGON

A dead girl is found floating in the River Teme at one of medieval Ludlow's mills, drowned under mysterious circumstances that only the most addle-witted could think was anything but murder.

Yet Stephen Attebrook, an impoverished knight and sometime deputy coroner, can spare no time to investigate this crime. He and his friend Gilbert Wistwode must pursue a more immediate threat — unknown ruffians traveling under the guise of bear baiters have kidnapped Stephen's niece, Ida, his estranged brother William's daughter, along with other young women across England.

Set against the backdrop of war brewing between King Henry III and rebellious barons arrayed about Simon de Montfort, a desperate chase of the bear wagon across England unfolds, reaching to the depths of London itself and far into Norfolk, as Stephen races to find Ida before she meets a fate worse than murder.

The Bear Wagon is Stephen's most complex and dangerous adventure yet.

Available at Amazon at
https://www.amazon.com/dp/B076337YRY

Made in the USA
Coppell, TX
15 September 2020